Dorothy's Derby Chronicles

WOE «OF» JADE DOE

Author/Illustrations Copyright © 2015 by Meghan Dougherty and Alece Birnbach
Cover and internal design © 2015 by Sourcebooks, Inc.
Cover design by Rose Audette
Cover and interior illustrations © Alece Birnbach

Sourcebooks and the colophon are registered trademarks of Sourcebooks, Inc.

Published by Sourcebooks Jabberwocky, an imprint of Sourcebooks, Inc.
P.O. Box 4410, Naperville, Illinois 60567-4410
(630) 961-3900
Fax: (630) 961-2168
www.sourcebooks.com

Library of Congress Cataloging-in-Publication Data

Dougherty, Meghan (Public relations consultant)
  The woe of Jade Doe / written by Meghan Dougherty ; with Karen Windness ; illustrated by Alece Birnbach.
       pages cm. -- (Dorothy's derby chronicles ; #2)
  Summary: "With the skating rink shut down and her flaky mom in town, Dorothy's life has become as jumbled as a derby jam. Not to mention the fact that bizarre occurrences befall anyone who enters the rink, and the girls think it might be haunted"-- Provided by publisher.
  (13 : alk. paper) [1. Roller derby--Fiction. 2. Roller skating--Fiction. 3. Haunted places--Fiction. 4. Mothers and daughters--Fiction. 5. Dating (Social customs)--Fiction. 6. Humorous stories.] I. Windness, Karen, author. II. Birnbach, Alece, illustrator. III. Title.
  PZ7.D74434Wo 2015
  [Fic]--dc23

                                    2015007491

Source of Production: Marquis Book Printing, Montréal, QC, Canada
Date of Production: June 2015
Run Number: 5004298

                         Printed and bound in Canada.
                         MBP 10 9 8 7 6 5 4 3 2 1

Dorothy's Derby Chronicles

WOE «OF» JADE DOE

Written by Meghan Dougherty with Karen Windness

Illustrated by Alece Birnbach

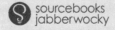

sourcebooks
jabberwocky

Introduction

In case you missed it...

Dorothy Moore, also known as the Undead Redhead, is the ring leader of the Slugs 'n' Hisses, a lively band of misfit roller derby girls. Dorothy stumbled—literally—into playing roller derby, a sport banned by her mother. While Mom is in Nashville chasing stardom, Grandma Sally, an ex–roller derby superstar and retired funeral director, introduces Dorothy and Dorothy's new middle school friends, Gigi and Jade, to roller derby.

Together, they recruit Lizzy, Dinah, Juana, Ruth, and Dee to form the Slugs 'n' Hisses and accidentally smack-talk their way onto the junior roller derby competition schedule when they barely have a clue about the sport. Meanwhile, the Pom-poms, middle school mean girls led by irritatingly perfect Alex, try to take down the Slugs through school pranks and antics. Grandma and Max, the Slugs' dashing young assistant coach, push Dorothy and her teammates to greatness.

As luck would have it, the Slugs find themselves in the championship bout on Halloween night. Besides playing the toughest team in the league, the Slugs are threatened by a destructive force from the Beyond. Mysterious disasters have plagued their practice headquarters, Galactic Skate, and stories emerge about Grandma's old teammate, Eva Disaster, who perished at the skating rink during Sally's time. The championship bout is haunted by a series of unfortunate incidents, including Grandma Sally being hauled off to traffic court and Dorothy's derby-hating mom showing up right before the big game.

Determined not to miss the bout, Dorothy and her little sister, Sam, attempt to drive Grandma's hearse, Dead Betty, with disastrous results. They are rescued on the roadside by an unlikely ally—nemesis Alex with her two dads, Jerry and David. The bout is an action-packed nail-biter, and the Slugs lose all hope of winning when Jade injures her ankle. Fortunately, Dorothy's quick thinking saves the day. To everyone's surprise, she calls in Alex to take Jade's place, and the Slugs secure the win in the final seconds of the game. As the crowd goes wild, Eva Disaster steps in to take her revenge. And that is where this story begins.

Chapter 1

"You okay, Dorth?" Max asked, squeezing Dorothy's hand.

Dorothy stared into Max's chocolate-brown eyes. Words weren't coming. From the tip-top of her curly red hair down to her hand-me-down roller skates, Dorothy was buzzing with delight. She wasn't even twelve yet, and she had just been kissed! She had thought the night couldn't get any better after coaching her team, the Slugs 'n' Hisses, to a win at the Halloween championship bout. But here she was, hand in hand with the boy of her dreams.

Floating on a cloud of bliss, Dorothy was barely aware of the roller rink under her feet or her nearby team chanting, "I'm a roller derby girl. Derby, derby, roller, yeah!"

And there was another sound too, like a squeal—but not a happy squeal. More like a metallic screech, actually. And it was growing louder. Dorothy's gaze shot upward and her bliss vanished, replaced instead with heart-pounding terror.

Suddenly, everything and everyone in the dimly lit, outdated Galactic Skate was moving in slow motion. The dusty ceiling fans ticked as slowly as the second hand on a clock. The people in the stands lumbered toward the door like molasses on the faded, star-patterned carpet.

"Get off the floor!" Dorothy screamed. "*Now!*"

Her team stopped chanting and turned to look at her with puzzled faces.

"Frappit," Dorothy said, dropping Max's hand. She rocketed toward her team, her arms waving frantically above her head. "Move it!" A second later, time was in hyperdrive.

"*You heard your coach!*" Grandma Sally yelled. Her tight, fishnet stockings made Grandma's thighs look like a pair of misshapen waffles. Unaware that her sexy nun costume was riding up dangerously high, she hooked Jade by the arm and pulled her toward the bleachers.

"Ouch, Grandma! Easy," Jade complained, hopping on one foot. "My ankle, remember?"

The next few seconds were a blur of confusion with the clack and swoosh of skate wheels, the cries of *"Run!"* from the few remaining fans standing in the bleachers, and above it all, a metallic banshee shriek growing louder each second.

In the chaos, Dorothy realized she had lost track of Sam. Cold fingers of panic wrapped around Dorothy's throat and squeezed. Her nine-year-old sister had been there just a minute ago, chanting and celebrating with her team. Where was she now? In the frenzy, Dorothy slowed way down, carefully scanning the people running past the rundown refreshment area and blackened popcorn machine and the restrooms with the groovy guy-and-gal signage. No Sam.

Then it happened. With a bang like a gun going off, the chain that held the giant disco ball to the ceiling snapped. Dorothy turned and watched helplessly as the ball fell. Time slowed again. It was like a horror movie version of the Times Square countdown on New Year's Eve—a glittering ball of death was plummeting toward the floor, and there wasn't a single thing Dorothy or anyone could do to stop it.

"*Sam!*" she cried desperately, but all she heard in return were the screams of her terrified teammates and shattering glass.

Chapter 2

Dorothy spun away just as a volley of mirror chips pelted her, painfully pricking the backs of her arms and legs.

From the bleachers, Dinah's thin arms waved spaghetti-like above her body. "*The sky is falling! The sky is falling!*" Dinah's small frame convulsed like a hummingbird that had just flown into a hornet's nest.

Lizzy clambered up the bleachers and shook the tiny girl by her shoulders. "Stop being illogical, Dinah! Everyone knows earth's atmosphere is composed of non-solid properties. The sky is most certainly not falling!"

Dinah was quiet for a full second before bursting from Lizzy's grip. "*Alien attack! The aliens are attacking!*"

"Calm yourself!" Grandma barked from the bottom of the bleachers across the rink from where Dorothy stood. "It was just that old disco ball coming off its chain." The room was nearly vacated, as she and the rest of her teammates drifted back to Grandma.

Dorothy turned her gaze to the ceiling just as a dark shadow whooshed over the broken chain, releasing a spray of sparks from the severed electrical cord. All of the hairs stood up on the back of her neck.

"*Grandma!*" she screeched, pointing a finger at the ceiling. "A...A..." Dorothy couldn't make the word "ghost" come out of her mouth.

"What is it, Dot?" Grandma asked, pushing through the other girls. "Are you hurt?" She turned Dorothy's shaking arm over in her hands, clucking her tongue like a protective mother hen. A mother hen in fishnet stockings and knee-high boots.

"Breathe, honey," she said, patting Dorothy's arm and letting it go. "I don't see anything here except a few scratches. You're not hurt."

"Well, *I'm* hurt," Jade said, falling heavily onto the bottom bleacher bench. She leaned forward and carefully tightened the white bandages that were looped around her swollen ankle. "Gigi pretty much ran me over, knocked the wind out of me, and left me for dead when the stampede started!"

"Wha…?" Gigi said, propping a fist on her round hip. "I did not run you over. I never even bumped you. You sprained your own stupid ankle, remember?"

Jade narrowed her eyes. "This isn't about my *stupid* ankle," she hissed. "You just about knocked me over, dummy. I nearly fell."

"Just now?" Gigi asked, confused. "I wasn't anywhere near you. You're the dummy."

"Am not," Jade returned.

"Are too."

Grandma whipped around. "Eva! Venom! Quit fighting!"

Jade and Gigi just stared at her blankly.

"Oh dear. Did I just call you…" Grandma's voice trailed off.

"Has anyone seen Samantha?" Dorothy squeaked.

Dorothy felt a light tap on her shoulder. "It's okay. I have her." Alex flashed her beauty-queen smile as Sam popped out from behind Alex's ruffly, pink-sequined skirt.

"You don't have to be a derby girl to move fast, you know," Sam said.

"Oh my gosh," Dorothy cried, pulling her little sister into her arms and squeezing her tight. After the big fight with Mom earlier that evening and the crash in Grandma's hearse, Dorothy had promised herself that she wouldn't let anything bad happen to Sam ever again. "I never would have forgiven myself if you had been…"

Sam giggled. "Squashed by a gigantic disco ball?"

Dorothy sighed. "Yeah, that."

Dorothy gave Alex a nod. "Thank you. You saved the day. Again." Once the feared class bully, Alex had helped win the championship by jumping in as jammer in the final minutes and then had saved Dorothy's little sister.

Alex shrugged. "No problem." She unsnapped her helmet and shook out her shiny, blond ponytail. Then she placed the helmet on Sam's head. "Give the jammer helmet back to Jade for me, okay? I'm going to go. My dads are waiting for me outside." And with a flip of her ponytail, she was gone.

"Attention," called a thin, wavering voice over the PA system. "Get out of the building *now*! The curse of Eva Disaster is baaack!"

"Darn it, Pops!" yelled Uncle Enzo, who was now on the rink examining the imbedded mirror ball and broken, shattered wooden floor. "Get off that intercom, you ol' coot." His bushy salt-and-pepper mustache wiggled nervously like a caterpillar on a hot car hood.

Galactic Skate had been passed down from generation to generation, from Pops's dad to Pops and then to Max's Uncle Enzo, who ran it with the help of Max.

"She's baaaaack," Pops crowed in a high, thin voice. The intercom made an ear-piercing squeal before going silent.

Most of the disco ball was lodged solidly in the

splintered wooden floor. Enzo's chubby face turned red, and he kicked the ball with his pointy leather shoe. A rainbow of hard plastic scales skittered across the skate rink, but the ball didn't move. Enzo said something under his breath and ran his hand over his greasy scalp.

"Pops is right about one thing," he said finally. "It ain't safe in here. Max!" he called. "Get these kids out of the building."

Max, Dorothy thought. She had forgotten all about him. Had she just left him standing under the disco ball?

"All right. You heard my uncle," Max said, rolling toward them from the other side of the rink. He caught Dorothy's glance briefly as he skated past, but there was no Max wink, no dimpled smile.

That kiss seems like a million years ago now, Dorothy thought.

Dorothy stared at the little brown curls at the back of Max's neck as he ushered the group past the bleachers, past the concessions area, and through the front door. Was he mad at her? She had left him standing under a ball of death after all. *What kind of girlfriend does that?*

Then again, "girlfriend" probably wasn't the right word. It was just one kiss. What does a kiss mean anyway?

Outside, the autumn night had turned chilly. Dorothy shivered and wished she had thought to bring a coat. She held Sam close to her. The parking lot of Galactic Skate was nearly empty, with the last handful of families walking to their cars. The clouds had cleared again and a perfectly round Halloween moon shone down on the building, illuminating the mural on the side of the large, square building.

The mural showed three disco-era roller skaters whooshing fast as if on a track: a young Grandma Sally with a huge, red Afro, a tall woman with brown skin and curly, bobbed pigtails, and a thin Asian woman with long hair that rippled behind her like a black flag. The last woman's mouth was a gaping hole of missing brick, her expression frozen in a silent scream. Eva Disaster.

Dorothy wrapped Sam tighter in her arms and let her gaze drop from Eva's screaming mouth to Eva's skates, which were exactly like Dorothy's except with gold wheels instead of white ones. "Do you think the curse is real, Grandma?" Dorothy asked, as she shuffled next to her grandmother.

Grandma had known Eva before her death. She had even been there the night Eva died.

Pushing back the sleeves of her nun's habit, Grandma ran her fake fingernails through her short, spiky pink hair. "I'm not sure, Dot. But I think there's a good chance we pushed Eva a little too far tonight."

Almost everyone had found their families and their rides and gone home. There would be no party, no pizza, and no sleepover. No celebrating the biggest win of Dorothy's life. She felt like everything she had worked so hard to accomplish had just shattered into pieces like that stupid disco ball.

Two police cars raced into the parking lot, sirens blaring, and peeled to a stop at the curb by the front entrance.

"Just great," Grandma said, fishing a pair of dark sunglasses out of her purse. "What?" Grandma asked, glaring at Dorothy and Sam over the top of her glasses.

"Had enough cop time tonight?" Dorothy replied.

Grandma had been at the police station dealing with speeding tickets most of the evening. She had missed most of the bout.

"Dot," Grandma said. "I've had enough cop time to last me the rest of my life."

"So they're not your boyfriends anymore, Grandma?" Sam asked.

"No, hon. Definitely not my boyfriends." Four policemen from two squad cars jumped out of their vehicles and ran into Galactic Skate.

Jade hobbled across the parking lot supported by her mom, Mrs. Song. "Nice helmet," Jade said, patting the top of Sam's head. "You guys need a ride?"

"Uh, yeah," Dorothy said. "Do you mind?" Grandma's car was sitting at the bottom of their driveway, the back bumper wrapped around a mailbox post. Dorothy felt horrible for wrecking the car, but Grandma had promised to be forgiving.

Jade's mom didn't answer. She was focused on the scene at the front entrance. Uncle Enzo was being interviewed by two police officers as a tall man in a brown suit made a big yellow *X* with police tape across the glass doors.

"Give me a moment," Jade's mom said, handing Jade off to Dorothy. "Be right back."

Dorothy watched as Mrs. Song smoothed her dark, shoulder-length hair and strutted confidently to Uncle Enzo. She unhooked her leather purse from her shoulder and produced a white business card. She placed the card in Enzo's palm, exchanged a few words with the man in the brown suit, smiled pleasantly, and returned to the group.

"All done," she said. "Now how about we escape this death trap?"

Grandma's shoulders stiffened. "Death trap?" she said. "My second home a death trap?"

"Uncle Enzo will fix it, won't he, Grandma?" Dorothy asked hopefully. Galactic Skate had started to feel like home to her too. A rundown home with carpet so gross that small children got stuck to it from time to time, but a home nonetheless.

Mrs. Song pressed a button on her keychain, unlocking

a shiny, black SUV with the words "Song Real Estate" printed on the side.

"Don't get your hopes up," Mrs. Song said as they climbed into the truck, Dorothy and Jade in the back and Grandma in the front passenger seat. The interior smelled like new leather. "That inspector said Galactic Skate will be condemned and bulldozed before you can say 'public hazard.'"

Dorothy gasped. "But it can be fixed, can't it?"

Mrs. Song shrugged and looked in the rearview mirror. "Enzo has a few months. But that would take a miracle. And a lot of money."

"How much money?" Grandma asked, her hand on Mrs. Song's.

Mrs. Song pulled her hand away. "Seriously?"

"Dead serious," Grandma said, leaning toward Mrs. Song. "How much to fix Galactic Skate?"

"Okay, okay. Let me think," Mrs. Song said. She rubbed her chin as the engine idled. "Well, there are the rotting floorboards, the crumbling ceiling, the rodent problem..."

15

Dorothy shuddered, remembering the mice in the basement storage room. She didn't want to meet them again.

"And don't forget about the ghost!" Sam said.

Dorothy's stomach lurched.

"Well," Mrs. Song said with a tinkling laugh that sounded like breaking glass, "you'll have to do your own ghost-busting, I think."

Dorothy shivered. She couldn't get the sound of that unearthly shriek out of her head, or the vision of that ghostly shadow whooshing across the ceiling.

After a few minutes of listening to the engine hum, Mrs. Song announced, "Fifteen."

"Fifteen dollars?" Sam asked. "We can do that. Right, Grandma?"

"Not fifteen dollars!" Mrs. Song laughed. "Fifteen thousand dollars! Minimum."

"Fifteen grand?" Grandma sucked air through her teeth. "You sure?"

Mrs. Song nodded. "Quite sure."

"Does Enzo have the money?" Jade asked.

Grandma shook her head. "No. Galactic Skate is bankrupt. Has been for a while."

Mrs. Song sighed. "Oh well. I do hope Mr. Enzo can find himself a good Realtor."

"Mom!" Jade groaned.

"Blossom, dear. It's time to face the facts. I have been very tolerant with you and your roller derby escapades, but Mommy cannot have you skating in a death trap."

"Can you please stop calling it a death trap?" Dorothy asked. Grandma's face was pale and gray. "It's just Galactic Skate, okay?"

"Garbage, garbauge," Mrs. Song said, shifting the SUV into drive. "Call it what you like. It's all trash. By Valentine's Day it won't be anything except an empty parking lot and a For Sale sign."

"Mom, please stop," Jade whined. "You're embarrassing me."

Dorothy balled her fingers into tight fists. "We aren't going to let Galactic Skate go without a fight. We'll find the money. We'll fix it. And we'll be skating here until… until we're old like Grandma."

"Old?" Grandma said, sounding like herself again. "Who you callin' old?"

"She didn't mean it like that," Jade said. "She just means we'll follow in your footsteps. Right, Undead?"

Dorothy followed Grandma's gaze as she turned to look through the back window at the mural. The three painted skaters seemed to be staring back at them.

Grandma sighed softly. "I sincerely hope not."

Chapter 3

"What are you smiling at, Mr. Pretty?" Dorothy asked. She thumped the penguin sticker on the front of her locker and the door popped open, school papers falling to the floor. It was Monday morning, and she was in a bad mood. She hadn't heard from Max since Saturday; Grandma was mad at her for wrecking the hearse; and thanks to an early-season snow shower, Dorothy had to walk to school instead of roller skate. And to make matters worse, her hair was now a big ball of damp, red frizz.

"Hey, Undead," Jade said, appearing behind Dorothy. "Trying out for clown club or something?"

"Jade!" Dorothy said, whirling around. "Where did you come from?"

"Like a ninja," Jade said, "even on crutches."

Jade was dressed in head-to-toe black. Even injured, her stealth and her petite, Goth warrior look were flawless. Her ankle brace was black. Her black T-shirt was a Jade original featuring a hand-drawn picture of her cat, Mr. Wrinkles, and her bare arms were covered in temporary tattoos. The largest design was a skull encircled by a ribbon that said *Trust No One*. Her crutches were crosshatched top to bottom with pink-and-black duct tape to match the team colors. The tops were covered in hot-pink faux fur.

"Is my hair really that bad?" Dorothy asked, turning back to her locker and peering into the mirror attached to the inside of the door. Her hair looked exactly like Grandma's Afro did on the Galactic Skate mural. Dorothy licked her palm and patted at the tangled curls.

"Gross," Jade said. "Don't lick it! Spit isn't going to fix that mess."

Dorothy turned and gave Jade the best of her worst scowls.

20

Jade coughed. "I mean, it's fine. Like, groovy, disco cool. Or, you know…"

Dorothy sighed and shut her locker. It was hopeless.

"Yo, Jade! Hopalong!" Gigi called, bumping her way through a knot of kids in the hallway. "I was calling you outside. Didn't you hear me?"

Jade's lips were pulled into a tight, flat line. "What do you want?"

"Sheesh!" Gigi said. "I was just wondering if your ankle was okay." Gigi was wearing a brightly colored headband that matched her formfitting floral top, which accentuated her curvy hips as she spun and turned her back to Jade.

Jade peered out at Gigi's back through a curtain of pink strands of highlighted hair. "So you care about my ankle now?"

"Dang, girl!" Gigi said, popping a fist onto her round hip and spinning back to Jade. "What is wrong with you? You act like I killed your ninja crime-fighting cat or something."

"Or something…" Jade grumbled. "More like you

killed my ninja jamming skills with that obvious shove."

Gigi opened her mouth, but Dorothy interrupted. "Are you going to P.E. today, Jade?"

Dorothy and Jade had Ms. Nailer's first-period P.E. together. Most of their team had been recruited from that class.

Jade shook her head. "Nope. No gym, just library duty." She fished a piece of carefully folded paper out of her pocket and handed it to Dorothy. "I was going to ask if you could give this to Ms. Nailer for me."

Dorothy unfolded the paper. "Nothing physical for two to three weeks? Really?"

"Yeah," Jade said. "That means no derby practice either."

"Oh no," Gigi said melodramatically. "How will we ever survive without our one and only jammer?"

Jade gave Gigi a nasty look.

"I can fill in," Alexandra said, appearing next to them. Alex was wearing a cute sweaterdress with matching leggings.

Jade's face went steely. "Listen up. I'll have you all

know that this is just a temporary thing. I'll be up and jamming again in two weeks. Tops."

"I know that," Alex said, flipping her silky, blond ponytail over her shoulder. "I'm not trying to steal your thunder or anything."

"Good," Jade said. "You remember that."

"But you know," Dorothy said, carefully refolding the doctor's note and tucking it into her shirt pocket, "we could use some extra jammers. Grandma's always saying our team is too small. And most teams have a lot of jammers, not just, uh, one."

Jade huffed. "We aren't most teams. We are the champs."

"Regional champions," Gigi said. "And only because Alex helped us. Remember?"

"Because of *all* of us," Dorothy said.

"Whatever," Jade said. "Doesn't really matter. If Galactic Skate is shut down, we won't have a team anymore anyway."

"What are you talking about?" Gigi demanded, confused.

"Jade's mom knows the extent of the damage," Dorothy said. "She thinks it could take fifteen thousand dollars or more to fix the rink. And Galactic Skate is totally broke. Beyond broke."

"Well," Gigi said, faltering. "We'll still have a team."

Jade rolled her eyes. "Oh? Where are we going to practice then?"

"Skate parks, parking lots," Gigi said. "There are lots of places to skate."

"In the snow?" Jade asked.

No one said anything. Jade had a point. Dorothy had tried to skate this morning. She hadn't even gotten to the end of the driveway before she was forced to give up. Skating in snow was impossible. And if the Slugs 'n' Hisses couldn't practice, how could they keep the team going?

"Have you guys thought about doing a fund-raiser?" Alex asked. "For Galactic Skate?"

"Fund-raiser?" Dorothy asked.

"Sure. We—I mean, the Pom-poms—do fund-raisers all the time." Until Saturday, Alex had been the leader of the Pom-poms, a club of pretty, popular, athletic girls and the sworn enemies of the Slugs 'n' Hisses.

Jade snorted. "You mean like that candy-eating contest for diabetes awareness?"

Alex shrugged. "Okay, so they weren't always the smartest ideas, but we made a lot of money. You guys should think about it."

"Yeah, but fifteen thousand dollars? In three months?" Jade shook her head. "Don't get your hopes up."

The halls were getting crowded now. And noisy. Dorothy could hear a group of boys talking loudly about the last football game and some girls debating about who wore the worst Halloween costume on Saturday. It was between Baby Yoda and the boy dressed as a gigantic roll of toilet paper.

"You sound like you want Galactic Skate to get bulldozed," Gigi said.

"Do not," Jade said. "I'm just being realistic. Fifteen thousand dollars is a lot of money."

Dorothy sighed. "It is a lot of money. And even if we do earn all that money, do you really think Eva is going to let us do roller derby at Galactic Skate?"

Jade nodded. "Undead is right, you know."

"So we get rid of the ghost too," Gigi said. "They do it all the time in the movies."

"Ha-ha-ha," Jade said, unamused. "Are you going to call an exorcist or something?"

"No," Gigi said, leaning in close to Jade. "But I'm not ready to give up on our team either. Are you?"

"Don't try me, Vicious," Jade growled.

"Whoa, whoa, whoa!" Dorothy said, sliding herself into the small space between her two friends. "Let's not fight, okay? I've already had to listen to Grandma yell at me all weekend."

"About the hearse?" Alex asked.

Dorothy nodded.

Gigi shifted her weight back onto her heels. "I thought G-ma was going to let you slide on that."

Dorothy scrunched up her nose. "Uh…she changed her mind when she saw Dead Betty."

Jade whistled through her teeth. "That bad?"

Dorothy nodded. "The whole back bumper has to be replaced. The muffler and exhaust-pipe thingies too. Grandma says Betty will be in the shop for months. And don't even ask me about the mailbox. Not pretty. I'm totally grounded."

"So you won't be at roller derby practice either?" Jade asked, seeming to perk up. "You could come to my house. We could…"

"That's one thing Grandma actually wants me to do," Dorothy said. "Derby practice."

"Oh," Jade said, her shoulders sagging over the tops of her crutches. "So what was the punishment then?"

"She grounded me from my cell phone."

"Ha!" Gigi said. "Your cell phone? You don't even use that thing."

"I know. I only have it for texting my mom. It doesn't even get Internet."

"So why did Grandma take it?"

"How should I know?" Dorothy said. "She's a weird old lady."

"Maybe Undead wants to text her boyfriend, Max," Gigi teased.

A ripple of hurt passed through Dorothy's chest. "Yeah," Dorothy said. "Maybe she does." She hadn't told her friends about her first kiss with Max. The whole thing felt all messed up now. She wasn't even sure if Max liked her anymore.

Just then the bell for first period rang.

"Go to class with me?" Alex asked, snatching Dorothy's backpack off the floor and handing it to her.

Dorothy hooked the backpack over her shoulder. "Uh, sure," she said, not feeling very sure at all. Before today, Dorothy wouldn't have thought Alex would have been caught dead talking to her at school, let alone walking her to class. It was a strange request, to say the least.

"Have fun," Jade said, cracking the first real smile Dorothy had seen from her that morning.

Easy for her to say, Dorothy thought as Alex escorted her through the crowded hallway. *She gets to go to the library. I have to deal with evil Ms. Nailer and the Pom-poms.*

28

Kids drifted aside for Alex like she was Poseidon parting the ocean, and Dorothy couldn't help but notice all the confused looks. Alex was everything Dorothy was not—movie-star beautiful, popular, naturally athletic, and graceful. Dorothy was all elbows, knees, and at the moment, frizzy red clown hair.

Although, Dorothy thought as they took a right at the office, *if Alex really is my friend now, maybe P.E. will be okay. The Pom-poms worship her, right? So maybe they'll stop hating roller skaters and be nice to the Slugs 'n' Hisses. We could all be friends. And skate together.*

Yeah, right, she thought miserably as she and Alex strolled past the cafeteria where something hot and sour was cooking. The scent reminded Dorothy of unwashed kneepads. *And maybe little pink fairies will fly out of Ms. Nailer's butt, and the lunch ladies will serve filet mignon for lunch. Not likely.*

HEELS b4 WHEELS

Chapter 4

"I have a cool idea," Alex said as they approached the entrance to the girls' locker room. "How about we get dressed in the bathroom instead of here?"

Dorothy's mouth said, "Okay," but her brain said, *All systems alert! Pom-pom trap! Pom-pom trap!*

Alex had said she was quitting the Pom-poms and joining the Slugs 'n' Hisses, but could she be trusted?

They continued down the hall and took a left into a doorway marked Girls' Room. It was empty except for the smell of strawberry perfume and hair spray.

"Why don't you take the big stall?" Alex said, slipping into the smaller one and locking the door.

Dorothy bent over and peered under the handicapped stall door. No feet. No bear traps either. Carefully, she pushed the door open. No bombs exploding, no buckets of hot tar pouring down onto her head. She crept inside the stall and looked down into the toilet bowl. No piranhas in the water. No tarantulas under the toilet seat.

"Can I tell you a secret?" Alex asked quietly through the stall wall.

Dorothy pulled her door closed and turned the lock. A poster on the inside door advertised Heels B4 Wheels: Roller Skating Danger Awareness Week.

Another stupid Pom-pom project, Dorothy thought.

"A secret?" Dorothy said. "Sure, Alex. What is it?"

"I'm…" Dorothy could hear Alex take a deep breath. "I'm afraid," she said finally.

Dorothy giggled. "Of what? I mean, you aren't afraid of anything. Are you?"

Alex made a sound that Dorothy guessed was supposed to be a laugh. "I'm glad you think so," Alex said, "but you know that thing I did on Saturday night?"

"Which thing? You mean the awesome skate dance or

helping us win the roller derby championship?" Dorothy laughed. "Man! The look on those Pom-poms' faces was…oh." Dorothy stopped cold. She now realized why Alex was afraid.

"Wait. You don't think the Pom-poms will strike back…" Dorothy started.

"Yes, I do," Alex said.

They finished dressing in complete silence.

Alex is the Pom-poms' leader though, Dorothy thought. *Everyone loves Alex. The Pom-poms can't be that mad at her just for roller skating.*

Dorothy looked at the poster again. *Join us in wearing heels and take a stand against the dangers of roller skating. Be smart. Don't skate.* In small letters at the bottom it said, *Brought to you by the Pom-poms, a skate-free community.*

Dorothy gritted her teeth. She ripped the poster off the wall, crumpled it into a ball, and tossed it into the toilet. "Don't worry, Alex," she said. "The Slugs 'n' Hisses won't let anything happen to you."

"Thanks," Alex said. "I know I can count on you guys."

Still, Dorothy was not looking forward to gym class.

Most of the Pom-poms would be there. And with Alex acting like her new BFF, Dorothy was sure the retaliation would extend to her.

As if reading Dorothy's mind, Alex said, "Hey, I have another fun idea. Why don't we ditch first period?"

"Seriously?" Dorothy asked, her heart skipping a beat.

"Sure!" Alex said. "I know a great hiding spot. No one will ever find us."

Chapter 5

Alex pulled Dorothy into a pitch-black room.

"Where are we?" Dorothy asked, her voice echoing in the darkness. Alex flipped a switch and a spotlight buzzed to life, illuminating a wooden floor and a jumble of half-assembled furniture.

"Backstage," Alex said, dropping her backpack next to the pool of light.

A heavy velvet curtain formed a wall to their right, and the spotlight cast eerie shadows on a half-built set: a four-poster bed with a Styrofoam mattress, a gigantic oven made out of cardboard, and a puffy, brown, headless turkey costume suspended from the ceiling by wires.

The tardy bell rang and Dorothy's chest tightened. "Nailer won't find us here, will she?"

"Don't worry," Alex said, taking a seat next to the spotlight like a fireside camper. "No one in class even knows we're at school, right?"

"Jade does," Dorothy said.

"Jade isn't going to class, remember?" Alex unzipped her backpack. "Besides, you don't think she would tattle on us, do you?"

Dorothy shrugged. "I don't think so." Jade had been acting really strange lately, but she wasn't a snitch. "I guess you're right," Dorothy said finally, taking a seat across from Alex.

It was chilly backstage, and goose pimples appeared all over Dorothy's freckled arms. "I still can't help thinking that Ms. Nailer will come looking for us."

Alex shrugged. "Well, if it makes you feel better, I know Ms. Nailer will be busy with the Pom-poms this morning. They're planning this big Heels B4 Wheels awareness project, and Nailer is helping them."

Figures she's helping them, Dorothy thought. Ms.

Nailer seemed to think everything the Pom-poms did was as magical as leprechaun farts.

"Why do they hate skating so much, anyway?" Dorothy asked.

"Because...*Priscilla*," Alex said. She said the name like she was spitting out a rotten pistachio.

"Which Pom-pom is that?" All those girls looked the same to Dorothy.

"Do you know the one with the big, white smile?"

Dorothy nodded. She knew the one. The girl looked like she had dentures, her teeth were so perfect.

"Well, it all started late last summer, before you moved here. Priscilla was roller skating—"

"She was *what*?" Dorothy said, shocked.

"Yeah," Alex continued. "Roller skating. At the park. And she tripped on a pebble and knocked out her two front teeth on a fire hydrant."

Dorothy gasped. The thought of it made her teeth throb.

"Yeah. They couldn't save the original teeth, so the dentist ordered her fake ones. There was a mix-up though, and Priscilla got someone else's teeth." Alex

36

giggled. "I shouldn't laugh, but those teeth were ridiculous. Huge! She looked like a cartoon squirrel.

"Anyway, they thought the right teeth would come in before school started, but they didn't. Priscilla had to come to school looking like that. She tried to keep her mouth closed to hide them and everything, but they were too big to hide. Really gigantic. You couldn't miss them. She had a lisp and everything."

Dorothy giggled. "I would have loved to have seen that!"

"Yeah, it was awesome. Anyway, teeth are her thing, right?" Alex continued. "And some of the kids started calling her 'Prithilla' and sneaking acorns into her backpack and stuff. She was really embarrassed, but more than that, she was angry. She got this whole thing in her head that roller skating did this to her. She's been on the skate-hate warpath ever since."

"But you're an artistic roller skater. Didn't that cause...problems?"

"I never told them about my skating. So it didn't matter."

PRITHILLA

"Well, they know about it now," Dorothy said.

"Yes, they do," Alex said. "Hey, I've been thinking about Galactic Skate. Why don't we brainstorm some fund-raiser ideas?" Alex pulled a ballpoint pen and a pink spiral-bound notebook out of her backpack.

"Sure," Dorothy said. Her hands and toes were numb with cold now. "But let me change back into my regular clothes first. I'm freezing. Is there a bathroom back here?"

"Not backstage. Why don't you just get dressed?"

"Here?" Dorothy said, looking around for a place to change behind the flimsy set pieces.

"I can turn around," Alex said, spinning around on her bottom so her back was away from the spotlight. She clicked her pen. "Okay. Number one. Bake sale. Can any of the Slugs 'n' Hisses bake?"

Dorothy kicked off her gym shoes. "I know Jade can. And Gigi's family has a diner. I bet she can bake too."

"Great," Alex said. "We could sell cupcakes at a refreshment table for the next school play. Mr. Macarini is doing *A Turkey Carol* for Thanksgiving."

That would explain the set, Dorothy thought. "I didn't

know Mr. Macarini taught drama." He was Dorothy's art teacher and her favorite teacher at J. Elway.

"Drama, art, and music," Alex said.

Dorothy stripped down to her tights and fished inside her backpack for her regular clothes. She was really glad Alex had turned around now.

"Number two," Alex said, tapping her pen on her notebook. "How about a talent show? The Pom-poms do one every year over Christmas break, usually on New Year's Eve. It makes a lot of money."

"Sure," Dorothy grunted, struggling to get her head into her blouse. Her hair had completely dried now and was a massive helmet of curls. "We have talents. We're (grunt) really talented," she said, tugging on her blouse. Dorothy pulled the shirt off again. *Frappit.* The buttons were already all undone. The collar opening wasn't getting any larger. She pulled the shirt on again and had it halfway over her head when she heard a giggle.

"Don't laugh," Dorothy said.

"What?" Alex said. "I was just trying to think of how we can get the talent show away from the Pom-poms."

Dorothy heard another giggle and pulled hard on her shirt. "Stop it, Alex. It's not funny."

"What's not funny?" Alex asked.

Dorothy pulled even harder. She tug, tug, tugged, but no matter what she tried, the blouse would not go over her head. *Frappit!* Dorothy thought. *My hair is just too big. I feel like a Chia Pet on Miracle-Gro.* She tried one last final pull, and the shirt came down an inch but wouldn't budge any farther. And now it wouldn't move upward either.

Dorothy heard more giggling. "Fine, Alex. I give up. Help me?" The blouse was squeezing her head now and it really hurt.

"I am helping you," Alex said. "These are really good ideas."

Just then, Dorothy was blasted with blinding white light. "Alex! Alex, what's happening?"

"*Run, Dorothy, run!*" Alex yelled.

Dorothy whirled left and then right, but couldn't see anything but the inside of her shirt. "Which way?" she yelled. But Alex didn't respond. All Dorothy heard was

40

a roar of laughter and the *koosh, koosh, koosh* of the velvet curtain being cranked open.

"I see London, I see France!" called a girl's voice.

"I see Dorothy's underpants!" another girl called.

Dorothy turned to run but tripped over her backpack and slammed into something hard. Something muscular.

"Stop it right there, Miss Moore," a familiar voice ordered. Strong hands held Dorothy by the shoulders, and old coffee breath filtered into her nostrils through the blouse fabric. "You've got nowhere to run, nowhere to hide. Ms. Nailer always gets her man."

Chapter 6

"How did you know we were here?" Dorothy asked, struggling against the wall that was Ms. Nailer.

Ms. Nailer cackled. "We? Is your invisible friend skipping class too? In her invisible undergarments, I suppose?"

More laughter.

At least Alex got away, Dorothy thought. Dorothy had promised to protect her, and this was certainly a start.

Ms. Nailer chuckled. "I suppose you need invisible friends right about now, don't you? Now that all your real friends are turning on you."

There were giggles from the audience.

Turning on me? "What do you mean?" Dorothy asked.

"Oh, nothing. Just that I would consider it wise to"—Nailer paused for emphasis—"trust no one."

Trust no one? Wasn't that what Jade's new tattoo said? Dorothy's stomach twisted. "You mean…Jade tattled on me?"

Ms. Nailer chuckled. "Now I didn't say that, did I?"

Jade? Not Jade! Dorothy thought. Alex she could almost believe, but Jade was her true friend. Wasn't she?

"And seriously, Dorothy," said Ms. Nailer. "Nice leopard print, but streaking is a very serious offense."

There were more giggles from the audience.

"Quiet, girls," Ms. Nailer said.

"I wasn't streaking! I'm stuck."

"Between a rock and hard place, it seems," said Ms. Nailer. "So how about you get dressed now so I can take you down to the principal's office."

"I can't," Dorothy said, wriggling inside her shirt.

"Don't sass me, Dorothy. Your radical nudist statement is not going to fly at J. Elway. We are a decent school with values and—"

"No!" Dorothy protested, wriggling like a fish caught in a net. "My shirt. I really am stuck."

"Oh. Ha! I see," Ms. Nailer said. "You really do have the worst luck."

Like I don't already know that, Dorothy thought. "Help me?"

"Okay, okay." Ms. Nailer yanked up on Dorothy's shirt.

"Erg!" gurgled Dorothy. "You're choking me!"

Ms. Nailer pulled down on Dorothy's shirt.

"*Ow!*" Dorothy screamed.

"All right, Pom-poms. Keep working on those posters," Ms. Nailer snapped.

So the Pom-poms were in the auditorium. *Figures*, thought Dorothy.

"I have a solution," called a girl's voice.

Dorothy groaned.

"Stay here," Ms. Nailer said, as if there was anywhere Dorothy could go. Her head was starting to go numb.

A moment later Ms. Nailer returned, accompanied by the click-clack of the Pom-pom's high heels. Dorothy heard the sound of a metal zipper.

"Step in," the Pom-pom said in an *eat this poisonous apple* kind of way.

"No way, nuh-uh," Dorothy said, scuttling backward. Whatever it was, Dorothy didn't want it.

"There are no other clothes here, so it's really your only option, Ms. Moore," Ms. Nailer said. "Walk through the halls in your underpants and tights, or take Priscilla's offer."

Priscilla? Dorothy thought. *Ol' Squirrel Chompers came to make my life miserable in person.*

"It's totally fine," Priscilla said. "Totally you, actually." More snickers.

Did Dorothy have a choice? Where did her clothes run off to? With a big sigh, she reluctantly lifted her right leg and felt something puffy and pillow-like slip over her leg.

Dorothy obeyed and then felt a cold metal zipper slide up her back. "Wait," Dorothy said. "This isn't that turkey costume, is it?"

"You look very tasty, my little butterball," Ms. Nailer said with a chuckle. She took Dorothy by what must have been a turkey wing. "Now march."

"Why are you helping the Pom-poms? Isn't that favoritism?" Dorothy asked before really thinking.

45

"They are a club, Dorothy," Ms. Nailer stated patronizingly, as from a rule book. "All clubs must have a teacher supervisor, and sometimes they may be given a pass from classes to complete projects." She might as well have ended with "So there."

"Hmmm…I guess Slugs 'n' Hisses could be a club, a fitness club," Dorothy thought out loud.

"Hissing slugs?" Ms. Nailer laughed. "Is that your gang name now?"

"*The Slugs 'n' Hisses, not Hissing Slugs!*" Dorothy yelled. She was really steaming now.

"How about we create a little contest for these two 'fierce' competitors?" Ms. Nailer snickered. "What do you think, Priscilla? The Slugs versus the Pom-poms?"

"Psh-shaw," Priscilla said.

"Prove it then," said Dorothy, as she yanked at the bottom of her blouse, managing to get part of one eyeball over the top of her collar. "Dare you to show us how fierce you are."

There was Priscilla, the stage lights illuminating her

46

dazzling white smile so that Dorothy was temporarily blinded. "So," Priscilla said, "How would you like us to beat you? Tennis? Basketball? Cheering?"

"Delicious," said Ms. Nailer. "I do love a good competition."

"How about something more, uh, challenging?" Dorothy asked, knowing the Slugs 'n' Hisses could never beat the Pom-poms at any of those things. "Like...roller derby?"

"Ha! Right!" Priscilla choked. "Are you serious? Really? As if, no way," she said. "I would die first."

She sounds just like my mom, Dorothy thought. "Okay," she said, trying to think of what else the Slugs could do. Gigi was a jam dancer and Alex was an artistic skater. Between those two, surely they could come up with a cool dance routine. "Dance competition. At the talent show."

"A dance fight? Any style we want?" Priscilla asked. A smug grin flashed across her face.

Dorothy shrugged her turkey shoulders. "Sure."

"Okay. And what do we get when we win?" Priscilla asked.

"*If* you win," Dorothy said, "you can keep all the talent-show funds...for whatever dumb cause you have going."

"We're already getting that," Priscilla said. "What else do you have?"

"We'll, uh...the Slugs will wear your Heels B4 Wheels shirts for a week."

"With high heels too?"

Dorothy groaned. She had worn heels once to a funeral and had tripped just as she got to the casket. She had never kissed a corpse before, and she never wanted to again. The whole idea of wearing heels left a really bad taste in her mouth.

"Heels or no deal," Priscilla said.

Dorothy sighed. "Sure. Heels too. But if we win..."

"That's a big if," Priscilla said.

"If we win," Dorothy continued, "all the money goes to save Galactic Skate."

"Galactic Skate? That filthy roller rink?" sputtered Priscilla.

"What do you care?" Dorothy said. Her head was

really starting to hurt from being stuck in her shirt collar for so long. If she didn't get cut out soon, the top of her head might die and fall off.

"Good point," Priscilla said. "There is absolutely no chance of you winning this."

"One more thing," Dorothy said.

"Isn't the money enough?" Priscilla said.

"Oh, let's hear what she has to say," Ms. Nailer said, enjoying every tense moment.

"If the Slugs win, the Pom-poms have to perform at halftime during our next roller derby bout."

"Perform? At a roller derby bout?" Priscilla's nose was crunched up like she had just smelled rotting sewage.

"Yes. And you have to do it in roller skates," Dorothy added, just to make it more interesting. She was enjoying watching Priscilla squirm.

Priscilla crossed her arms over her chest. "No! I said no skates!"

"It's just a bet," Nailer said. "Pom-poms are a shoo-in. Just shake on it, Priscilla."

"Then it's a deal?" Dorothy asked.

Priscilla huffed, but reached out and shook Dorothy's turkey wing anyway. "Fine. Whatever," she said. "But be warned, we will not make this easy for you Slugs."

"Bring it!" Dorothy said, turning on her turkey heel and strutting toward what she hoped was the stage exit. She did her best to look fierce, not an easy thing to pull off in a turkey costume. One second she was shaking her tail feathers and the next she was flying through the air, a tumbling, bouncing ball of turkey meat rolling down the aisle of the auditorium.

Dorothy scrambled up and adopted her best turkey strut into the hallway. She was thankful that only a few students were out of class. Thinking suddenly about how Grandma would handle something embarrassing like this, Dorothy stood straight, clucked proudly, and waved as if she were in a parade all the way to the nurse's office.

Chapter 7

By the time she headed to gym class, Dorothy had an after-school detention slip. Fortunately, when she peeked her head into the gymnasium, P.E. was almost over and Ms. Nailer and the Pom-poms were nowhere to be seen. It was just the regular, old Slugs 'n' Hisses running laps, minus Jade and Alex, of course.

Dorothy laced up her Converse sneakers and began to run, her shoes squeaking rhythmically on the polished linoleum. The sky still looked gray through the windows, but at least the snow seemed to have stopped. Her mind wandered back to the stage. How embarrassing. And she couldn't believe Jade had thrown her under the bus like that.

Tattling didn't seem like Jade's style. Alex, maybe. For all Dorothy knew, Alex was still the leader of the Pom-poms and the whole thing had been a big Pom-pom joke. Then again, maybe Alex was smart enough and fast enough to get away. And Dorothy was, well, Dorothy. She always seemed to be getting herself into a mess. What had she been thinking, signing herself and her team up to compete in a dance fight against the Pom-poms?

Just look at us, Dorothy thought as her teammates jogged their way around the track. Childlike Dinah was skip-hopping and swinging her arms like she was delivering a basket of goodies to Grandma's house. Lanky Geekzilla, Lizzy, was swerving on and off the track, her nose in *A Star Fleet Cadet's Complete Guide to Cosplay*. Big Ruth, a.k.a. Rolling Thunder, wasn't rolling—or running—at all. Hands on her knees, she was huffing and puffing by the side of the track, her face pink and sweaty.

Dee Tension, muscular and tough looking, wasn't running either, but she didn't look like she'd ever started. She was just leaning against the brick wall, picking her teeth with a toothpick. Soft and round Juana, the seemingly least athletic, appeared to be the only normal runner. She was also the shyest person Dorothy knew. Would Juana be able to perform onstage? In front of an audience? *What a mess*, Dorothy thought. Sure, these girls could skate, but could any of them dance? Dorothy already knew she was a terrible dancer. *What was I thinking?*

Juana slowed as she ran past Dorothy. "Where were you?" she asked softly.

"Nowhere. Just late," Dorothy replied, too embarrassed to tell Juana the truth.

At the end of the school day, Dorothy reported to Mr. Macarini's classroom for detention. The sun had finally come out from behind the clouds, and the spacious art room was filled with yellow light. It should have made Dorothy happy, but it didn't. She stood in the doorway debating whether she should sit down or make a run for it.

Mr. Macarini was at his desk, staring out the window. He was combing his handlebar mustache with a tiny comb. His long, dark, curly hair was pulled back in a ponytail. Dorothy thought he might actually be hand-some if he just shaved off the hedgehog mustache.

Two other students were in detention besides Dorothy. Dee was sitting in her usual spot writing "Dee Tension was here" in big letters across the top of her desk. And the other kid was… Well, he was looking at Dorothy. He was a good-looking boy with chiseled features and shoulder-length blond hair. She hadn't seen him before, but she was still pretty new to the school. There were a lot of kids she didn't know.

He flipped his long bangs and gestured for Dorothy to take the seat next to him.

"Hi," Dorothy said, once she had settled in.

"Angel," the boy said, extending a hand.

Dorothy could feel her face go hot as they shook hands. No one had ever called her "angel" before.

He flipped his hair again and leaned in close. "So, like, I just moved here from California," he whispered, "and dude! What is up with the snow? It is like totally frigid."

54

Dorothy giggled. He was funny. And the California thing explained why he was wearing flowered shorts, a loose-fitting tank top, and tennis shoes with no socks.

"So…like, I told you my name," he said. "What's yours, dude?"

"Dorothy," she said, realizing "Angel" must be the boy's name, not a compliment. How embarrassing.

"Dorothy?" Angel asked. "Nice, dude. So totally *Wizard of Oz*. So, like, what are you in for?"

"Uh," Dorothy said, not really wanting to tell Angel about her bra and panties. "Ditching class?"

The boy nodded approvingly. "Wicked."

"And you?" Dorothy asked.

"Duuude!" Angel said. "So, like, did you know that inline skating on school property is like totes illegal here?"

"Uh, totes," Dorothy said. "New rule. No wheels on campus." The Pom-poms had pushed that stupid restriction through last month.

Angel shook his head. "Dude…like, *no bueno*."

"Totally," Dorothy agreed. "So you roller skate?"

"Sure, man," Angel said, flipping his hair again.

"Doesn't everybody? I'm like into quads, blades, long board, skateboard, surfboard. I mean ocean surfing, obviously. You totally can't surf here."

Dorothy giggled.

"And, like, dude! This snow totally kills my skate flow."

"Mine too," Dorothy agreed. "Hey! Why don't you come to...?" She fell silent. She was going to invite Angel to Galactic Skate, but what was the point now?

"Quiet, criminals," Mr. Macarini said, setting down his tiny mustache comb. "Zip the chat and do some homework, *por favor*. I'm missing an air-guitar contest at Hill of Beans Coffee Cantina, so do me a favor and make good use of this time."

Dee stood up. "Uh, Mr. M., I don't have any homework, so can I go now?"

"Sit down, Dee. If you had gone to your English class, you'd have homework," Mr. Macarini said. "I thought you weren't skipping class anymore."

Dee shrugged and sat down again. "I forgot."

"And what about you, Dorothy? You're the roller

derby coach now, remember? Since when does the coach ditch class?"

"Dude! Roller derby coach?" Angel said, impressed.

Dorothy looked down at her desk. "Slugs 'n' Hisses have hit a…uh…rough patch." She hated to disappoint her favorite teacher.

"Hmmm," Mr. Macarini said. "Well, I hope you can repair things soon. Don't tell Ms. Nailer, but I think roller derby is good for you and the other girls. Like Dee here."

"And, dude! Like, totes cool! Do you need any more referees?"

"Thanks," Dorothy said. "Maybe? I'll keep you po—"

Dorothy didn't finish her sentence because the classroom intercom started blaring, "Mr. Macarini! Mr. Macarini! Please meet animal control at your car immediately. We have another…situation."

Mr. Macarini sighed and slowly rose to his feet. "Not this again. Okay, class. I'll just be a minute," he said, pulling a coat out from under his desk. He stopped in the doorway and turned to look at Dorothy. "But I suppose this means you'll be making your exit now, won't you?"

She sighed. "I don't know if I'll have a choice." The last time she was in detention, she had been unwillingly dragged through the window by Jade and Gigi and rescued by Grandma.

"Look, Dorothy," Mr. Macarini said in a whisper. "Between you and me, I think you've learned your lesson. No more ditching class, okay?"

Dorothy nodded.

"And, Angel? Dee? If you two accidentally get sucked out the window too, well I'll let that slide this time. I'd really like to get to that contest. I've got some rad new chords I've been dying to show off." Mr. Macarini pretended to play an electric guitar, moving his fingers up and down the invisible instrument's neck in a wild series of unheard notes. He finished his solo by swinging his right arm around and around like a spinning windmill blade.

Dee raised her fist in rocker salute. "Rock on, Mr. M.!"

"Like, dude!" Angel said.

"Shhh! Quiet now," Mr. Macarini said. "This is just between the four of us. Oh, and say hello to that grandmother of yours, okay, Dorothy?"

58

"You know about my grandma?"

"Everybody knows about your grandma," Mr. Macarini said with a chuckle. "I can't wait to see what she's hidden in my car this time."

"Be careful," Dorothy said.

"You too," Mr. Macarini replied, and he was gone.

She barely had her homework back in her backpack when she heard a *knock-knock-knock* at the window. A single face was pressed up against the glass. Alex.

Dorothy walked over to the window and pushed it upward. A blast of cold air rushed into the classroom, causing goose bumps to appear all over her arms.

"What do you want?" Dorothy asked, eyeing Alex with suspicion. Alex had left her on the stage in her underwear.

"I'm really sorry you got caught," Alex said. "I thought you were going to get away. Why didn't you run?"

"I was stuck in that shirt! And totally blind!" Dorothy said, her arms folded across her chest.

"Stuck? I had no idea!" Alex looked genuinely sorry. "Well, I'm making it up to you now. And you'd better come quickly. Mr. Macarini will guess it's a stuffed skunk in no time, and then we'll all be in trouble."

"Who's 'we'?" Dorothy asked. Dead Betty was in the shop, and from what Dorothy could tell, Grandma had lost her driver's license, probably because of all the speeding tickets. No getaway car, no rescue, right?

Alex flipped her silky, blond ponytail and smiled. "You'll see."

Chapter 8

Dorothy crawled through the window and crunched through the snow to join Alex at the curb where a pink Vespa scooter with black racing stripes was waiting for them. Attached to the side of the scooter was a coffin on wheels. Sitting astride the scooter was Grandma, wearing a black bomber jacket, a pink helmet, and old aviator-style goggles.

"What is this thing?" Dorothy yelled to Grandma over the sputtering motor.

"A Vespa!" Grandma said, snapping the goggles onto her face.

"I know what a Vespa is," Dorothy said. "What is this thing?" She gestured to the coffin.

Grandma shook her head. "Don't tell me you've never seen a casket sidecar before, Dot? Hop in!"

"It's fun," Alex said, swinging herself gracefully into the front of the coffin.

Dorothy sighed and climbed in behind Alex as Grandma leaned over and fished out two helmets from behind Dorothy's seat.

"Safety first!" Grandma said, plopping the helmets onto Dorothy's and Alex's heads.

"Since when are you interested in safety?" Dorothy asked, clipping the helmet under her chin.

For an answer, Grandma revved the engine and putt-putted out of the parking lot.

When Dorothy looked back over her shoulder, she saw Dee and Angel waving to them from the curb.

She scanned the parking lot and located Mr. Macarini and a couple of animal-control officers having a good laugh over the stuffed skunk perched on the roof of Mr. Macarini's car.

"Hey, G-Grandma!" Dorothy yelled, once they were out on the road. It was bitter cold in the sidecar.

"Where's Sam?" Elementary got out an hour before J. Elway. Had Grandma just left her nine-year-old sister at home alone?

"She's at the funeral home with Morti and Auntie Venom."

Morti was Grandma's Boston terrier, but Auntie Venom? Had Grandma bought a snake? "What is Auntie Venom?" Dorothy called.

"My old derby wife. She'll be babysitting you while I catch up on some things with the, uh, authorities." At that, Grandma gunned the engine and hit a pothole, covering Dorothy in icy slush. She was so cold now that she couldn't even feel her fingers.

"You have a wife?" Alex asked excitedly.

Grandma laughed. "Yes and no, hon. She wasn't my real wife. A derby wife is like your roller derby BFF. Like Jade and Gigi. We watched each other's backs back in the day."

Jade and Gigi are more likely to stab each other's backs right now, Dorothy thought.

Once Alex had been dropped off at her house,

Grandma and Dorothy went back to the funeral home. The house was toasty warm, and delicious smells were wafting from the kitchen. Definitely not Grandma's cooking. Grandma's idea of a gourmet meal was a piece of processed cheese between two pieces of white bread that had been burned into unrecognizable blackness with a clothes iron.

As they were about to walk into the funeral home, Dorothy grabbed Grandma's arm.

"I'm just curious. How did you and Alex, of all people, end up as the getaway team?" Dorothy asked.

"Alex showed up at the funeral home after school, all winded like she ran the whole way here, and begged me to spring you. How could I say no? I do love a good detention heist."

"Honey! I'm home!" Grandma called, putting her helmet and goggles on a coat hook.

A tall woman with coffee-brown skin and short, curly hair turning silver at the ends appeared from the kitchen.

She was wearing a pot mitt on her

right hand and took it off to shake Dorothy's still-freezing fingers. "Pleasure to meet you, Dorothy," she said. "I'm your grandma's friend, Vanessa, but you can call me Auntie. And I have just the thing to warm you up. I hope you like clam chowder."

"I've never had it, but it smells awesome," Dorothy said, already liking Auntie Venom.

Sam skipped out of the kitchen wearing an apron like a superhero cape. "I was in charge of the awesome," she said.

Soon dinner was on the table: warm, crusty home-made bread and a big bowl of steaming, creamy soup. It was delicious.

"So you were Grandma's derby wife?" Dorothy asked after her second bowl of soup. She had spent her lunch period in Ms. Nailer's office, and watching the P.E. teacher eat a whole bowl of tuna salad, while wearing most of it on her mouth, had taken away Dorothy's appetite. The clam chowder tasted like heaven.

Auntie chuckled. "So you've seen the Galactic Skate mural."

"You're on the mural?" Sam asked.

Auntie put two fists at the back of her head like pigtails.

Dorothy's mouth fell open. Auntie was the third skater!

"We were like the Three Musketeers back in the day, weren't we?" Grandma said.

Auntie sighed. "Until Eva took things too far."

"Now, now," Grandma said. "You know we don't like to talk about that."

"Eva ruins everything though," Dorothy said. "Did you know she's haunting us?"

"She tried to kill us with a disco ball," Sam said cheerily.

"She doesn't want us to do roller derby," Dorothy added.

Auntie clucked her tongue. "I can't say I believe all those ghost stories, but I have to admit, that sounds like her. If Eva can't play, she doesn't want anyone else to either."

Dorothy suddenly felt a little sick to her stomach. "Can I be excused?" she asked.

Grandma nodded. "Why don't we call it a night? You girls will get plenty of time with Auntie in the next few weeks."

The words echoed in Dorothy's head. *If Eva can't play, she doesn't want anyone else to either.* That description sounded way too much like someone else she knew. Someone she wasn't sure she could trust anymore.

Chapter 9

On Saturday, Dorothy called up her team and they met at the skate park around the corner from Juana's house. During the week, all the snow had melted and it was a perfect, sunny day. One of those warm November afternoons with blue skies and puffy, white clouds that almost made you forget that it was freezing just a few days before.

Unfortunately, Jade's foul mood was raining on everyone's parade.

"Perfect weather, don't you think, Jade?" Dorothy asked as she laced up her skates.

Jade didn't even look up from her sketchbook—new

fashion designs, from what Dorothy could tell. "There won't be many more days like this," Jade grumbled. "Soon it will be snowy and icy and miserable. Then what?"

Gigi stood up and rolled out onto the smooth cement track. "What do you care, Hopalong? It's not like you can skate anyway."

Jade dropped her sketchbook and crutches and lunged at Gigi, hopping on one foot and air karate-chopping, but Dorothy snagged her by the back of her sweatshirt and dragged her back to her seat while Gigi skated off.

"Not worth it, Jade," Dorothy said. "You're going to reinjure that ankle, and you want to be able to skate in another couple weeks, don't you?"

Jade gave Dorothy a sour look and picked up her sketchbook. "In the snow?" she grumbled.

"Stop worrying about the weather! We'll earn enough money to fix Galactic Skate. You'll see."

Jade didn't look up from her drawing. "Sure we will."

"Look, Jade, we're doing a bake sale at the play on Friday, a talent show on New Year's Eve, and, oh!

I forgot to tell you. Grandma and Auntie Venom are putting together a geezer bout over Thanksgiving break. They've already got most of their old team signed up."

"Old ladies? Doing roller derby?" Jade burst into a fit of maniacal laughter. "That's the stupidest thing I ever heard!"

Dorothy gave Jade her best angry face. "You've seen Grandma skate, right?" Everyone knew Grandma still had all her old derby skills.

Jade wiped a tear from her eye. "Yeah. But Grandma is, uh, different."

"I'm sure the other geezers are different too. I mean unique...I mean... You know what I mean."

Jade was still laughing when Sam skated up. "Since Jade is broken, can I be the jammer first?"

Dorothy nodded. It had been Grandma's call to let Sam play on the team since the Slugs were so short on players. "Go ahead," Dorothy said.

Sam squealed and zipped back onto the makeshift rope track. She did a lap, zipping past Dinah Mite and Juana SmackHer, and squeezing through the tiny space between Geekzilla and Rolling Thunder as they warmed up and practiced blocking.

"Dang," Dorothy said, watching her little sister easily outmaneuver Gigi's classic Booty Vicious bump. "That girl can skate!"

"Whatever," Jade said, slamming her sketchbook closed. "She's just a kid. It takes maturity to be a good jammer."

Dorothy pulled her coach whistle over her head and skated off from the step. "Then maybe you'll be a good jammer someday too, Jade."

"I know you're trying to replace me!" Jade called. "You can't replace me. I'm the fastest..."

Dorothy stopped listening, focusing instead on the wind in her face and the rhythm of her wheels on the pavement. Her first lap was a little rough; she fell twice and tripped over her own feet more than a few times, but by the second lap, she was feeling confident. What a relief to be skating again. Nothing could make her happy like skating could. No wonder Jade was so grouchy. Being stuck in an ankle brace had to be horrible. After a few more laps, Dorothy decided she owed her friend

71

an apology, but when she got to Jade's spot, she found it was empty.

She felt a tap on her shoulder and whirled around to see Angel staring down at her. "Dude! Like, what are you doing here?" He was wearing his flowery shorts and a T-shirt, kneepads, and blades.

"Angel!" Dorothy said, blushing. "I'm, uh, here with my roller derby team."

"Dude!" Angel said, giving Dorothy a high five. "I'm, like… Those roller chicks are, like, so totally wicked!"

"Pretty wicked." Dorothy had to agree, watching her team do another lap.

Gigi skated up and did a fancy hockey stop in front of Angel. "Introduce me to your friend, Dorothy," she said, batting her eyes.

Dorothy did, but had to look away. Gigi was acting all weird and giggly. She knew Angel was cute and nice, but this was just awkward. Was this how she acted around Max? Dorothy looked back and saw Gigi

flirtylicious

72

smiling, complimenting Angel on his Rollerblades and asking how he learned those perfect scissors. Dorothy had to admit that she probably acted a lot like that around Max. It made her feel embarrassed and lonely at the same time. She missed Max.

"So you're going to referee for us, right, Angel?" Gigi was saying.

"Can I? I mean, like, no way! That would be so totally radtacular!" Angel replied.

"Great!" Gigi said. "And look! Here come the Peanut Butter Jammers now!"

"You called the Peanuts?" Dorothy asked, turning to watch a group of elementary-age kids skate up. They weren't much bigger than Sam.

"Vicious!" Dorothy whined. "The Peanuts totally kicked our butts last time we played them. This is embarrassing!"

"I heard that," said the leader of the bunch, a skinny girl with freckles named Strawberry Shortstack. "But if you guys can't beat us, you for sure won't be able to beat the Steamroller Punks."

"Steamroller Punks?" Dorothy asked.

73

"Why would we play them?" Gigi added. "We already won the championship, remember?"

One of the Peanuts shook her head. "You guys really are new, aren't you?"

"Be nice, Killer Barbie," Shortstack said, shooting the little girl a disapproving look.

Strawberry turned back to Dorothy and Gigi. "Okay, look. You won the regional championship, right? But now you go to state. And the team you have to play is not going to be as easy to beat as the Cheerbleeders."

What? Dorothy thought. The Cheerbleeders had almost destroyed them during the championship bout. Slugs 'n' Hisses had won by the skin of their teeth.

"How can the Steamrollers possibly be harder than the Cheerbleeders?" Gigi asked.

"Because the Steamrollers play dirty. Real dirty. That's why they got kicked out of our league. When your team took their place, they joined another league. Now you play against them."

"Uh, so what do you mean by 'play dirty'?" Dorothy asked.

"Like, don't leave your skates unattended before the game, dirty."

"And don't let them near your drinking water, dirty," said Killer Barbie.

"And watch out for their sharp teeth," Shortstack added. "Those girls bite. And I don't think they've had their shots."

"Oh," Dorothy said with a shudder. "That kind of dirty."

"And that's not the worst part," Strawberry said.

Gigi's fists were on her hips. "What's worse than biting?"

Shortstack leaned in close. "They have it out for you."

"Out for us?" Dorothy exclaimed. "Why?"

"Because you took their spot in the lineup, duh," Barbie said.

Gigi folded her arms over her chest and stared worriedly at Dorothy. "Come on. It's not like we got them kicked out of the league," Gigi added.

Shortstack shrugged. "We know that, but that's not how they see it."

Killer Barbie rubbed her hands together. "And now they have something to prove."

"So what do we do?" Dorothy asked with a shrug in Gigi's direction. She felt panic rising in her chest.

"For one," Strawberry said, "make sure you play the Punks on your turf. If you play anywhere but Galactic Skate, some of you will probably not be skating again." Strawberry looked over her shoulder at Barbie. "Hey, remember what they did to Hamburger Girl?"

"Hamburger Girl?" Gigi said. "What happened to Hamburger Girl?"

Barbie narrowed her eyes to slits. "Let's just say her name wasn't Hamburger Girl before we played the Steamrollers."

Dorothy cringed.

"For another thing," Strawberry continued, "you'll need more players. How many do you have now?"

Dorothy turned and looked at her team. Alex was at the center of the rink, executing a tornado-speed ballerina spin. Dee Tension was skating around the track in the wrong direction, arm extended. It was only a matter of time before she clotheslined one or more of the other Slugs.

"Currently?" Dorothy asked. "Nine. But Jade will be better soon, I think."

"Nine!" Strawberry said.

All twenty Peanuts broke into laughter.

Shortstack finished laughing and sighed. "Sorry. It's just, no one plays roller derby with nine players! Not only that, but you won't be eligible to play at state unless you fill up your roster."

Just then, Sam skated up. She was breathing heavily but not winded. "Did I hear someone say we need more players?"

"Yeah," Dorothy said. "We do."

Sam pulled a cell phone out of her sweatshirt pocket.

"Where did you get my phone?" Dorothy asked. She hadn't seen that thing in a week.

"In Grandma's underwear drawer."

"Ew!" Dorothy said. "What are you doing in her underwear drawer?"

"Spy stuff. Not a big deal. Can you guys be quiet now? I gotta talk to someone."

Sam skated away to make a call. When she came back, the Slugs played a round against the Peanuts. Even though the Slugs had improved since their last bout, the Peanuts had improved too. Slugs lost.

Jade had come back and was sitting in her old spot. She appeared to have given up on her drawings; the sketchbook was gone. "You guys stink without me!" she yelled.

"Nice cheering, Jade," Gigi said. "Did you make that cheer up yourself?"

As the Slugs and Peanuts got in position for another period, a group of five kids rolled onto the skate rink. They were about Sam's age and all had straight, dark brown hair and lightly freckled toast-brown skin, and they were wearing matching T-shirts that said "The Quints."

"These are my friends from school," Sam said. "They are quintuplets. Meet Penny, Polly, Pepper, Piper, and Paige," she said, pointing at each kid as she introduced them. "All *P*s!"

Dinah squealed and did her happy-clap dance. "You guys are identical twins? That is totally awesome!"

Piper rolled her eyes. "We're not…"

"Identical," Paige finished.

"Can we do roller derby now, Sam?" Pepper asked.

"I've got the need for speed," said Paige.

79

"Wait here a second," Dorothy said, hooking her sister by the elbow. "I need to talk to Sam. Alone."

Once Dorothy had Sam out of earshot, she whispered, "You didn't just invite the Quints to join our team, did you?"

"They can at least try out, can't they? Their mom plays adult roller derby! They just moved to town. These five have actually been playing roller derby for two years. They just haven't picked a junior team yet."

"No way, Sam!" These kids aren't any bigger than... than you!"

Sam looked hurt. "I'm not so small, you know," she replied. "And besides, the Quints can skate. And you said we need skaters."

Dorothy shook her head. The Slugs were a middle school team. Sure, they had made an exception for Sam, but Dorothy didn't want to be babysitting a bunch of elementary school kids.

"Just look at them!" Sam said, pointing past Dorothy to the skate track.

Dorothy turned to look and her jaw dropped. The

Quints were on the track now, skating in tight formation like a pack of wolves on roller skates. They flowed around each other effortlessly, reading each other's minds, offering whips, and launching each other faster and faster around the track.

Even Jade was on her feet now.

"Holy cow!" Gigi said.

"Can we keep them?" Dinah squealed.

"But, but we don't even know if they're housebroken," Jade said.

"Who cares?!" Dorothy said. She blew her whistle, and the Quints peeled to a stop in front of Dorothy. "Welcome to the Slugs 'n' Hisses!"

"Game on!" Shortstack said.

Chapter 10

On Saturday, the night before *A Turkey Carol* was set to perform, Dorothy, Gigi, Jade, and Dinah met at Gigi's parents' diner to make cookies. They hadn't planned on inviting Dinah to help, but she had found out, and Dorothy didn't have the heart to say no. Gigi's mom was running the restaurant while Gigi's dad was out of town. Mrs. Johnston said the girls could use the kitchen after the last customer went home, and in the meantime, she put the girls to work. Dorothy and Dinah filled water glasses, Gigi cleared tables, and Jade, whose ankle was still hurting, sat at the counter and rolled silverware into napkins.

It was nine p.m. by the time the last group of diners left, but the girls weren't tired. They had helped themselves to the soda machine while they worked, and each had drunk at least one liter of Mountain Rage Cola. Dorothy was so buzzed that her teeth where chattering. Dinah was in full-on hyperdrive, babbling incomprehensibly and darting around the kitchen fetching ingredients like a cartoon squirrel.

"Focus, focus, focus," Jade said, her hands shaking as she measured and dumped flour cup by cup into the big electric mixer. "We can't afford to mess these up."

"She's right, totally right," Gigi agreed, tossing whole sticks of butter into the mixing bowl. "These ingredients weren't cheap. Gotta pay Mom back. Gotta make some money too."

"Gotta save that place with the roller skates and the pizza and stuff," Dorothy added, cracking egg after egg into a glass bowl at warp speed.

"*Sugar!*" Dinah bellowed as she overturned a whole bag of sugar into the big mixer.

"*Whoa*, Dinah!" Gigi said, wrestling the sugar bag

away from the hyper girl. "That's enough. That's good. Perfect. Just right."

"Is it? Is it magically delicious?" Dinah asked, clapping her hands together like a windup monkey.

For some reason Dorothy found this hilarious and started giggling. "Magically delicious!" she said, bursting into laughter. She could barely catch her breath because she was laughing so hard. And the harder she tried to stop laughing, the harder she laughed.

Gigi giggle-snorted. "Stop laughing, Undead!" she demanded and giggle-snorted again.

"Did you just snort?" Jade asked, doubling over with a peal of laughter.

"I...*giggle snort*...can't stop...*giggle snort*!" Gigi cried.

Dorothy was laughing so hard now that she couldn't breathe. Her stomach ached.

"I need to pee!" Jade cried, hopping up and down on her good foot.

"Me...*giggle snort*...too," Gigi said.

Dorothy was still laughing too hard to talk, but she crossed her legs and nodded in agreement.

Gigi hooked Dorothy and Jade by the arm. "Potty break!"

"I'm good. I'm fine," Dinah said. "I'll work on the cookies while you go."

Dorothy wanted to suggest that someone stay behind to keep an eye on Dinah, but she still couldn't talk. Besides, she really, really had to pee now.

There was only one stall in the women's room so they had to take turns, and they all ended up having a major giggling fit while looking at themselves in the bathroom

mirror—their hair and faces were caked with flower and butter and sprinkles. Then they smelled it.

A baking bomb had exploded in the kitchen. Choking, the girls waded through gray smoke pouring from under the mixer. Horrible grinding and squealing screeched from the machine. Gigi raced to the mixer and yanked the electrical cord out of the wall. The mixer whirred to a stop, but the squealing sound continued.

Dorothy gasped. "Where's Dinah?"

"Whiddle help pweeze?" Dinah squealed from some-where in the smoky haze.

"What the…?" Gigi asked. Dinah was standing next to the mixer with a beater hanging from her tongue.

Dorothy ran to the little girl. "Dinah! Your tongue! Poor thing. Are you okay?"

"*Waaaaah!*" Dinah cried, tears showering from her eyes.

Jade snatched the end of the beater and yanked it off Dinah's tongue.

"*Oow!*" Dinah cried, grabbing her tongue.

"Serves you right," Jade barked. "How did you get your tongue stuck in the mixer, anyway?"

"I thinished making the cookieth," Dinah lisped, "and I...I justh flicked the bweethers."

"You flicked the bweethers?" Gigi asked, her fist on her hip.

"No," Dinah said, fishing a beater out of the metal bowl and holding it to her swollen tongue. "Llithing. Thee?"

"All I see is a broken mixer," Gigi huffed.

"She did roll out the dough though," Dorothy noticed, glad that there was a bright side to this disaster. Four large sheets of lightly floured brown dough were ready to be cut and baked.

Gigi pressed a finger into a sheet of dough and shrugged. "Not bad, but still..."

"Oh no!" Jade said, sucking air through her teeth. "Don't look now, but I think Dinah's tongue is bleeding."

"Bleeding?" Dorothy asked, her head swiveling automatically to look at Dinah. "Oh, she is blee..." Dorothy said, her voice slurring and knees buckling at the sight of blood. She willed her eyes to look away, but it was too late. Her body crumpled and everything went black.

When Dorothy came to, she was lying on the floor looking up at Gigi, Jade, and Dinah. "What happened?"

Gigi's fingers were on Dorothy's wrist, taking her pulse. "Dinah happened, that's what," she said.

"How long was I out? Are the cookies okay?" Dorothy asked. She could smell warm baking smells.

"The cookies look fine," Jade said. "They're almost cool enough to decorate. I don't know if we have enough, though."

"Enough for what?" Dorothy asked, pulling herself up onto her elbows.

"We did the math," Gigi said. "Between the supplies and getting that mixer fixed, we'll have to sell every last cookie for a minimum of seven dollars each to make any profit at all."

"Seven dollars!" Dorothy said. "No one's going to buy a cookie for seven dollars."

Jade shrugged. "What choice do we have?"

"Ith for a good cauth tho, wight?" Dinah lisped. Her tongue was wrapped in gauze and she was holding a zip-lock bag of ice to it. "Bethides, they're gourmet!"

"Gourmet? Oh no," Gigi said, all the color draining out of her face. "Oh no, oh no, oh no…"

"What did you put in the cookies?" Jade demanded, her nose an inch from Dinah's. "Spill it, Dinah!"

"Don't thweat it," Dinah said, smiling from ear to ear. "They're dewithuth! I sthwear!"

Chapter 11

The following night, Dorothy, Gigi, Jade, Alex, Lizzy, Ruth, Juana, and Dee met in front of the school auditorium an hour before *A Turkey Carol* started.

The Quints and other cast members in black-and-white Pilgrims' outfits, animal hides, ponchos, and feather headdresses were running around taking care of final show details.

Lizzy looked up from counting cookies and pushed her glasses up her long nose. "Shameful costume inaccuracies," she said. "Did they research anything about Thanksgiving? Or Charles Dickens, for that matter?"

Alex taped a crepe-paper flower decoration to the front of the table. "It's just a play, Geekzilla."

"We're not going to see it anyway," Gigi added.

Dee perked up the collar of her black leather jacket. "I don't even wanna see it. Plays are for sissies."

"That's not true," Dorothy said.

"Has anyone seen Dinah?" Jade asked, reaching into her jean jacket pocket for a Sharpie. Jade's jacket was bedazzled with silver studs, and she had painted a black widow spider in roller skates on the back. "How am I supposed to label these cookies when I have no idea what's in them?"

"Dinah's in the play," Ruth said with a giggle. "She's got the lead role!"

Juana swept the dark hair out of her eyes. "She is the turkey."

"The turkey?" Dorothy asked.

Gigi groaned. "Appropriate."

"That's it. I'm done," Jade said, throwing down the marker. She snatched her skull-and-crossbones messenger bag and hobbled to the door.

"Don't go, Jade!" Dorothy called. "The cookies look incredible!"

"Sorry, Undead. I've got better things to do than this," Jade called, pushing the door open with her big, clunky walking cast. "Good luck with Dinah's mystery cookies." And with that, she was gone.

"Good riddance," Gigi said.

"What do you mean by that?" Dorothy asked.

Gigi shrugged. "Jade's been all moody ever since she hurt her ankle. I'm starting to think she wants us to fail."

"Fail?" They heard high-pitched tittering. Priscilla and her pack of bleached-blond Pom-poms had sauntered out through the auditorium doors and had been standing nearby the whole time. "That *is* what you're best at, isn't it, Hissing Slugs?"

Alex was instantly on her feet and in Priscilla's face. "What do you want, Priscilla?"

Priscilla smiled. Her teeth were blindingly white. "Haven't you heard? The Pom-poms are doing a bake sale too."

"Tonight?" Dorothy asked.

"Uh-huh," Priscilla said with a devilish smirk. "Right over there." She pointed in the direction of the ticket-booth windows. As if on cue, the metal security window on the left began to roll upward, revealing a stack of white boxes and a sign that said: "You're too fat! Buy a pie for the skinny homeless people. Only seven dollars each."

"Seven dollars!" Lizzy exclaimed. "We can't compete with that pricing."

"Oopsie!" Priscilla said, feigning innocence.

The other Pom-poms giggled.

Alex's face had turned red. Her manicured hands were balled into tight fists. "You're doing this on purpose!" she spat out.

Priscilla shrugged. "I guess you should have thought about that before you double-crossed the Pom-poms, hmmm? Come on, girls," she said, turning on her heels. "Let's go sell some pies."

"Don't worry," said Gigi, patting Alex on the shoulder. "You're too fat so buy a pie? That is such a dumb idea. I'm sure our cookies will sell just fine."

As audience members began filing through the lobby, the Slugs quickly discovered they were wrong. Nearly every person walked over to the bright signs and fake smiles beamed by the Pom-poms. Every time someone bought a pie, Priscilla winked at Slugs 'n' Hisses.

For seven dollars you could buy a cookie or give a pie to the homeless shelter. Despite the stupid sign, the pies were selling. And the cookies were not. As soon as the play began, the Pom-poms packed up and filed out, waving at the team as they left.

Slugs 'n' Hisses manned their table throughout the play in hopes someone would walk out to the bathroom and buy a cookie.

They could hear cheering and clapping coming from the auditorium, and then the people filed out. The show was over, and they had only sold two cookies. Pity buys from Mr. Macarini.

"Can I eat this now?" Ruth asked, picking up a skate-shaped cookie with pretty pink frosting.

Gigi shrugged. "Go for it, Thunder. I'm hungry too."

Dorothy and the rest of the girls joined Ruth in

picking out a cookie. Dorothy unwrapped a skull-shaped one and took a bite out of the little pink bow. She immediately spat it out. "What the…?"

"Holy…!" Ruth said, giggling and covering her mouth with her hand. "This cookie is…super hot!"

Gigi ran to the trash and spit. "Turkey? Who puts turkey in cookies?"

Just then Dinah bounded out of the auditorium side door in the turkey costume. "Thruprise!" she said, flapping her turkey wings.

"Dinah!" Dorothy said, wagging her skull cookie in Dinah's direction. "What did you put in these things?"

"Oh! That one ith, uh, peanuth butter and sthweet pickles."

"*Peanut butter!*" Lizzy bellowed. "Did you even stop to think about allergies? You could have killed someone with these!"

"Oh, thorry," Dinah said, looking really dejected. "I dinith know."

Ruth giggle-panted. Sweat was pouring down her now-pink face. "What's in mine?"

"Jalepenyoth!" Dinah said, clapping her turkey wings together.

"Jalapeños?" Juana asked, smacking her head. "*Está loca*."

"So much for the bake sale," Gigi said. She picked up a tray of cookies and headed for the trash can.

"Wait!" Alex called. "Don't throw those out. Let's save them for school. I think it's about time we offered the Pom-poms a peace offering. Don't you?"

Gigi laughed and patted Alex on the back. "Spoken like a true Slug."

Dorothy giggled too. "Alex, I think we're going to like having you on our team."

Chapter 12

"That was your boyfriend, Dorothy," Grandma said, hanging the phone receiver back on the wall.

It was Sunday, and Dorothy and Sam were eating Grandma's infamous burned-cheese sandwiches.

"Ha-ha, Grandma," Dorothy replied, not looking up from her charred lunch. "I don't have a boyfriend, remember?"

Grandma patted Dorothy's head like she was a lonely dog. "You and Max on the fritz?"

Dorothy stood up so fast that her chair tipped over. "Max? That was Max on the phone?" She hadn't seen or heard from Max since the championship bout. "What did he say, Grandma? Does he want to see me?"

Grandma laughed. "Calm down, Dot! He just wants us to come over to Galactic Skate."

"He does? What for?" Dorothy's heart was racing now.

"So we can say good-bye, hon."

"Oh no!" Dorothy said. "He—Max is leaving?" Hot tears sprang into her eyes.

"Oh, honey," Grandma said, putting an arm around Dorothy's shoulder. "Not Max. He wants to give me—us—a chance to say good-bye to Galactic Skate." Grandma looked out the window and sniffed.

"But we had until January first! We planned fundraisers. They can't tear it down now!"

"No, they're not bulldozing yet. But Max says there's been more trouble."

"Like Eva trouble?"

Grandma nodded. "Enzo is going to a lunch meeting with a Realtor in an hour. Max suspects the land will be on the market sooner than later. He says if we come now, we can pick up some mementos without ruffling any feathers. You want to say good-bye, don't you, Dorothy?"

Dorothy nodded. "Can I invite the team? They'll want to say good-bye too."

"Sure, hon. I don't see why not."

Dorothy called everyone, but the only ones who could come right away were Jade, Gigi, and Dinah.

If anything, Galactic Skate looked worse than ever. Chunks of wall were missing, ceiling fans hung from electrical cords at odd angles, and scorch marks ran up the wall next to the pizza kitchen.

The skate floor was unchanged from Halloween night. The bleachers were still up and the disco ball was still down, embedded in the center of the skate floor and surrounded by orange cones, yellow tape, and a million broken mirror bits.

Max came out of Enzo's office carrying two old shoe boxes filled with black-and-white photos, trophies, and newspaper clippings. "Take what you want, Sally," he said, setting the boxes on top of the broken air-hockey table. "I have a couple more in the basement. Why don't you help me get those, Dorothy?"

Dorothy blushed as Max took her hand.

"I'll help!" Gigi offered, bumping past her and heading for Pops's rental desk where the basement entrance door was located.

"We got it, Vicious," Max replied. "I, uh, actually need a minute alone with Dorth, okay?"

Dorothy's face went hot as Gigi raised an eyebrow and then grinned.

So maybe Max isn't mad at me after all, Dorothy thought. Her hand started to sweat a bit in Max's. She hoped he didn't notice.

"Ready?" Max asked, pushing open the door to the basement. The smell of rotting wood and moist dirt was so strong that Dorothy could taste it. A dim yellow bulb lit their way, but the stairs were seriously creaky, each one giving off a ghostly moan. Dorothy's fear was quickly replaced by embarrassment as Dinah, Grandma, Gigi, and Jade started singing "Dorothy and Max sitting in a tree…" from somewhere above.

"Max?" Dorothy whispered. "Can I ask you a question?"

They were at the bottom of the stairs now, and Max turned and looked into Dorothy's eyes.

"Are we…" she started. "Are you my, uh, boyfriend?" Dorothy swallowed hard, praying that she wouldn't get sick and lose her cheese sandwich all over Max.

Max chuckled. "Well, I am a boy, and I am your friend, if that's what you mean."

"Oh," Dorothy said, dropping her gaze.

Max reached out and lifted Dorothy gently off the last step. But instead of setting her on the floor right away, he held her tight against his chest. "I really, really like you. Okay?" he said, his breath warm and cinnamon-y on her lips. Dorothy felt her body melting in his strong embrace.

From upstairs, Dorothy could hear them still chanting, "K-I-S-S-I-N-G."

Dorothy closed her eyes and leaned forward, lips ready, but instead of feeling Max's soft, warm lips against her own, her teeth snagged on Max's shirt buttons as she was dropped to her feet.

Max wasn't looking at her. "But let's just be friends. Okay, Dorth?"

Dorothy felt like she had been kicked in the gut. She

willed herself not to cry, but the tightness in her throat was unbearable. "But why?" she managed to croak. "After the bout, you…the kiss, I thought…" Her voice trailed off.

"It's not you, Dorth. It's me, okay? It's just been really stressful around here. My uncle is totally freaking out, and things keep falling apart and catching on fire, and…" Max sighed. His hand was on her shoulder and his eyes were soft. "You understand, don't you, Dorth?"

Dorothy nodded, but she didn't understand. Why did any of that matter if they really liked each other? She could help him, support him. Love conquers all and everything. At least it always did in the movies.

"And besides," he continued, "you're only eleven and…"

Dorothy tightened her jaw and stepped back away from Max. "I'm almost twelve, you know!"

"Right. I mean, I know. And I'm fourteen now."

"So?"

Max shrugged. "And so we have time. That's all."

Dorothy's arms were folded tightly over her chest. "Sure. Time. Great." She knew he could hear anger and disappointment in her voice, but she couldn't help it. *We have time?* It was an excuse, just like millions of excuses her mom was always using to shut her up. "You'll like the funeral home," she had said. "It's only temporary," she had said. Yeah, right.

"Cheer up, Dorth," Max said, taking Dorothy's chin between two fingers. "I have something to show you. Something cool."

Max crept over to one of the wooden storage shelves and removed a warped cardboard box, setting it on the floor.

"Come look!" he said.

Dorothy peered into the vacant space and saw a faded color photograph in a dusty frame, tacked to the wall by a rusty wire and nail.

"Who are they?" she asked. The photo was a faded color shot of the big mural outside, freshly painted by the looks of it. At the bottom of the mural were three men standing arm in arm and grinning from ear to ear. The man on the left was twice as big as the other two guys. His shirt collar was unbuttoned, revealing a pile of gold chains draped over his hairy chest.

The man in the middle was short and round. A stubby cigar was clenched between his teeth, and he was wearing a black fedora hat, a black pinstripe jacket with matching pinstripe shorts, black socks, and flip-flops. The man on the right was thin and gaunt. He was wearing a plain gray suit, and his hair was dark and curly like Max's.

Max pointed to the handwritten scrawl at the bottom of the photograph. "To Flip-Flops, from your loyal business associates, Moochie and Popcorn."

"That's Pops," Max said, gesturing to the thin man on the right.

"You mean that old, wrinkly guy who rents out the skates?" Dorothy asked.

"That old, wrinkly guy is my grandfather."

"Oh," she said. *Open mouth, insert foot.* "I didn't know. I mean, he's really nice and everything."

Max laughed. "No, he's not. You just think he's nice because he's sleeping all the time. He's actually pretty grouchy. And paranoid. He really believes that whole Eva curse thing."

I believe it too, Dorothy thought, but she decided not to mention that. "So who are the two other guys?"

Max shrugged. "Moochie and Flip-Flops, I guess."

Dorothy leaned in to get a better look. "You know, this is a really weird place to hang a photo."

"That's what I thought too," Max said. "Hand me the picture. I want to show you something else."

Dorothy lifted the little photo from the nail on the wall and found a light switch behind it.

"What's this switch for?"

"You ready for this?" Max asked, reaching for it.

Dorothy stepped back and nodded.

The moment the switch was flipped, the bookshelf swung open on squeaky hinges.

Mice scampered out of the dark behind the wall, and Dorothy shrieked involuntarily.

"Shhh!" Max said, putting his hand lightly over her mouth. "I don't want anyone to know we found this."

When the mice were gone, Max stepped into the dark room, and a dusty, stained glass chandelier flickered to life, the old, yellow lightbulb glowing dimly.

It was a small room, not much bigger than the storage area they had been standing in, but a million times more refined. The walls were covered in dark, luxurious wood paneling. The room smelled of old cigar smoke and dust. Lots of dust. And in the center of the room was a round poker table covered in mouse-bitten green felt, surrounded by six wooden chairs. Everything was covered in dust, but under the translucent blanket of gray, Dorothy could make out several sets of abandoned playing cards. At the center of the table was an orange plastic pumpkin, one of the kind kids use for trick-or-treating. She could see money sticking out of the top of the pumpkin, mouse-nibbled dollar bills mostly.

"Whoever was playing must have left in a hurry," Max said. "Otherwise they would have taken the money."

Dorothy crept in to get a closer look and felt something crinkle under her foot.

"What's this?" she asked, bending over to pick up a tattered, yellow flier. She was still holding the framed photo of Moochie, Popcorn, and Flip-Flops, so she set it on the table before blowing dust off the faded paper.

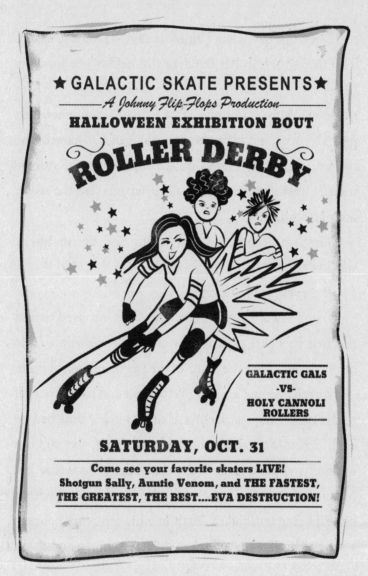

"Does this say what I think it says?" Dorothy asked. The flier shook in her hand as she held it out for Max to see.

Before Max could take it, a cold shadow whooshed past Dorothy and blew the paper out of her hands. She rushed to grab the flier as it was sucked into the storage room, but she ran into the wall panel and sent the secret door crashing shut.

Dorothy kicked the door again and again, but it wouldn't open.

"*We're trapped!*" she cried.

"Calm down, Dorth," Max said. "We just need to find the switch. There's got to be one on the inside too." He began to feel along the seam where the opening had been.

Dorothy turned away from the wall and forced herself to breathe. She was feeling claustrophobic and had to calm down. *Stay calm*, she said to herself, focusing on the pretty colored glass of the chandelier. She would not imagine the walls closing in. She would not envision herself being crushed to death in a hidden room beneath a haunted roller rink. She would stay positive and think good thoughts. "On the bright side," she said aloud, "at least we have light."

Just then, the lightbulb winked twice, dimmed, and then died, casting the room into total darkness.

"*Maaaaxxxx?*" Dorothy squealed, her entire body crawling with spidery fingers of fear.

She felt a gentle hand on her shoulder and Max's warm breath at her ear. "Has anyone ever told you you're cursed?"

She laughed nervously. "Yeah, well…it could be worse! At least the building isn't on fire, right?"

"Don't say things like…"

Dorothy didn't hear the rest of the sentence. A loud, screeching alarm began to sound from somewhere above.

Her heart pounded out of control. "That isn't what I think it is, is it?"

Max sighed. "You have a real gift, Dorothy. You know that? Now how about helping me find that switch before we're toast."

Chapter 13

Dorothy felt along the smooth wooden wall as the alarm blared on.

She could hear Grandma yelling from the top of the stairs, "Dorothy! Max! Get your tails up here. Something's on fire!"

So Galactic Skate is on fire! Dorothy thought. She spun around so fast her ankles crossed and felt herself falling forward as she tried to untangle her legs. Before she could stop herself, her head hit the wall with a hard thump, hard enough that the wooden wall panel moved. It sunk and slid forward under her weight like some kind of oversized button.

"You found the switch!" Max said as the door creaked open.

Dorothy would have crashed to the floor if Max hadn't grabbed her by the hand and dragged her, stumbling, out of the hidden room and up the rickety stairs, two by two.

The alarm grew louder and louder, and when they reached the top step, they could barely make out Grandma and Sam through all the gray smoke.

"*Everybody to the back door!*" Max ordered.

They were joined by Gigi and Dinah as they ran to the exit, but where was Jade? Hopefully outside already. Even on crutches, Jade was fast.

The smoke was dense near the back door, and the hallway was blocked by a dark figure bouncing up and down on its bottom like a frog.

"A leprechaun!" Dinah squealed. "Dibs!" She took a running leap and tackled the figure.

"*Oof!*" it said. "Get off me, Dinah!"

"You can't fool me!" Dinah replied, pinning her leprechaun to the floor.

Max reached into the open window on the left side of

111

the hall and turned on the neon Hot Pizza sign. He flipped another switch, and Dorothy heard the whir of a fan.

"*Whoops!*" Dinah said as the smoke began to clear, rolling off her captive.

Jade sat up. "I'm not a leprechaun!"

"Too bad," Dinah yelled over the alarm. "We could have used that pot of gold."

Max marched past Jade to crack open the back door. Bright light and fresh air rushed into the hallway.

He looked angry. "What happened here?" he demanded.

"I was…just putting out a fire," Jade explained.

Dorothy noticed a jean jacket on the floor beneath Jade. Burn marks scarred the sleeves, and the jacket was smoking slightly.

Gigi threw her hands in the air. "With your butt?"

"With my coat!" Jade said, bouncing up and down to demonstrate.

Max shook his head. "That still doesn't explain how the fire started."

"You started this?" Gigi yelled just as the alarm stopped and Galactic Skate was silent again.

"I…no. It was an accident," Jade said.

"No wonder you wanted to come with us today," Gigi grumbled. "Did your Realtor mom put you up to this?"

"Are you accusing me of trying to burn down Galactic Skate?" Jade asked, getting to her feet.

Gigi shrugged. "You said it, not me."

"Well, I wasn't. Okay? I was just"—Jade bit her lip—"smudging."

"Smudging?" Gigi said, confused.

"That's not like poodle scooting, is it?" Dorothy asked. Morti was always dragging his stinky little butt around the funeral-home carpet. It was gross.

"No! This." Jade bent down and lifted her jacket. Sitting in the center of the burned circle was a cigar-shaped bundle of pale green twigs, tied together with white twine. One end was charred black and still smoking slightly.

"Since when did you start smoking?" Gigi asked. "I swear. It's like I don't even know who you are anymore."

"No, sillies," Dinah said, lifting the bundle by the cool end. "It's sage. You burn it to get rid of evil spirits."

Jade's gaze dropped to the floor, and she nodded in agreement. Her shoulders were trembling; she looked frail and cold.

"That still doesn't explain this carpet," Max said. "What am I going to tell my uncle?"

"Promise not to laugh?" Jade asked, her eyes large like a guilty child's.

Max shook his head. "Believe me, I will not laugh."

"Eva did it," Jade whispered. "She…just came out of nowhere like a cold shadow, and the next thing I knew, the smudge stick was on the floor and the carpet was on fire."

An icy shiver zipped up Dorothy's spine. What Jade was describing was exactly like what she had felt in the basement. Could that have been Eva too?

Jade's eyes were distant. "We have to get rid of her, you know. We have to get rid of Eva Disaster."

"Right now, I have to get rid of smoke and evidence," Max said, gesturing to the carpet. "So you all better leave

114

before my uncle gets back here with his Realtor."

Realtor? Dorothy thought. *Jade's mom?* She looked at Jade, and Jade looked away.

Aha! So it *was* Jade's mom. She was pushing Enzo to sell. And maybe they were faking all this Eva ghost stuff to scare everyone away. Like some kind of real-life *Scooby-Doo* episode.

"Good-bye!" Grandma called, hugging the walls of the smoky hall, tears rolling down her wrinkled cheeks. "I'll miss you, old friend."

Dorothy set her jaw. *I will not let Eva or Jade or anyone else take away Galactic Skate.*

Chapter 14

Later that night at the funeral home, there was a knock at Grandma's door.

Dorothy looked through the peephole, expecting to see Uncle Enzo or the police, or both. Max had promised to cover for them, but they had left him with a lot of smoke and a serious burn mark in the carpet.

But it wasn't Enzo or the police. It was Mom.

Dorothy pulled the door open. "What are you doing here?" she asked.

Mom was wearing a rhinestone leather jacket, a cowboy hat, and cowboy boots. "I thought you'd be excited to see me," she said, stepping inside and giving Dorothy a hug.

"I am," Dorothy lied, wriggling out of Mom's arms. "I just…wasn't expecting you."

Mom looked confused. "You weren't?"

Grandma appeared from her bedroom. "Jeez, Dolly! Haven't you heard of a telephone?"

"My name is Holly now, Mom. Holly Mackerel. And I did leave a message," she said, giving Dorothy a hard look. "This isn't funny, Dorothy. You texted me and said I should come, so I came. Do you have any idea how long I've been on the road?"

Dorothy gritted her teeth. "Give me a second," she said, storming out of the room. She came back a moment later with her cell phone in one hand and Sam in the other.

Sam escaped from Dorothy's grasp, flung her arms around Mom's waist, and gave her a big squeeze. "You came!" she said. "I knew you would!"

"Give me that," Grandma said, snatching the cell phone away from Dorothy. "I thought I grounded you off that thing." She turned back to Mom. "Anyway, I'm glad you're here."

"You are?" Mom looked stunned.

"Sure," Grandma said, opening up the closet and pulling out her leopard-print skate bag. "You can babysit the girls. I've got geezer practice tonight, and you know how wild those old girls get. No place for children."

"You're doing roller derby?" Mom asked, astonished, her fists on her hips. "Still?"

Grandma unzipped the bag and emptied out the contents: elbow pads and kneepads, six or seven mouth guards, a pair of skates, and a helmet with a shotgun decal on the side. "So you've got Dorothy and Sam tonight, or not?"

Mom looked down at her cowboy boots.

Grandma looked up at her and shook her head. "Don't tell me you had other plans."

Sam's happy face melted like neglected ice cream.

Figures, Dorothy thought, anger rising into her chest. *And she wonders why I'm not happy to see her.*

"It's just…" Mom said, still staring at her boots, "I made a date."

Dorothy's heart dropped into her stomach. Mom dating? Never a good thing. Not ever.

Grandma straightened up and grinned. "Well, all righty then," she said. "Is he cute?"

Mom blushed. "Well, yes. He's handsome. And successful too."

Grandma leaned against the wall and raised an eyebrow. "You're not dating the manager at Gino's Pizza again?"

"No, Mom," she replied, sounding annoyed. "I broke up with Kyle when I was fifteen. This is someone…new. He's a music producer. Well, he works for a music producer."

"From here?" Grandma looked confused.

"From Nashville, Mom. We drove here together, if you must know."

Dorothy sighed. *Less than a month in Nashville, and she's already got a boyfriend. Gross.*

Grandma pushed away from the wall and started piling her equipment back into her skate bag. "You are serious about that singing career, aren't you?"

"Of course I am. And Jim thinks Holly Mackerel is gonna be a huge star," Mom said, slipping into a country drawl.

119

"I can't believe you're still going by that stupid name." Grandma groaned.

"It's not stupid," Mom said.

"And this Jim guy?"

"Jim Schwartz," Mom said. "And he's not stupid either."

"So he's your"—Grandma paused— "manager?"

Mom blushed. "Yeah, something like that."

Grandma zipped the bag shut. "Oh dear," she said. "I know that look. You're serious about this guy, aren't you?"

Mom's hands were on her hips. "So what if I am?"

Grandma stood. "If you are, you better introduce him to the girls."

"I…I was…planning to," Mom said reluctantly.

"Great. Then we'll set two extra plates for Thanksgiving dinner tomorrow. Vanessa's making her famous fried turkey."

"You're still friends with Auntie Venom? You haven't changed a bit, have you?"

"Nope, not a bit," Grandma said. "Speaking of which, Auntie's going to be here soon to give me a ride to practice. Are you going to take the girls with you on that date or not?"

"*Pleeeeease!*" Sam begged, hanging off Mom's arm.

Dorothy looked at Grandma. "Can I just stay with you? I'll be good," she pleaded. Dorothy would rather take her chances with a room full of crazy grandmas than with Mom and her new boyfriend.

Mom's lips were a tight, thin line. "Fine," she said. "Sam can be my chaperone tonight. We're going out for a nice dinner and then a movie, but you wouldn't be into any of that, would you, Dorothy?"

Dorothy knew Mom was trying to make her feel jealous. "I'm into roller derby," she said flatly and stormed out of the room.

Chapter 15

"So, where's the practice?" Dorothy asked from the back seat of Auntie's white Chevy Malibu. There was a delicious-smelling tray of crab puffs on the seat to her left and Grandma's skate bag to her right.

Auntie stopped for a traffic light and glanced over to Grandma, who was applying a layer of hot-pink lipstick.

Grandma smacked her lips together. "No place special, Dot. Just this little hole-in-the-wall skate joint I know."

"Oh no," Dorothy said breathlessly. "Not Galactic Skate!"

Grandma didn't say a thing.

"But it's all locked up, Grandma. Remember? We can't get in."

"You sure about that?" Grandma said. She reached into her blouse and produced a silver key hanging from a shoelace string.

"Where did you get that?" Dorothy asked, not really wanting to hear the answer.

"Chillax, Dot. I just borrowed it from Enzo's office. I'll put it back eventually."

Dorothy didn't say anything for the rest of the drive. She was so nervous about going back to Galactic Skate that she stuffed crab puff after crab puff into her mouth until they pulled into the pothole-ridden parking lot.

A wave of relief washed over Dorothy when she saw there were no other cars in the lot. "Guess that means practice is canceled," she said. And a good thing too. She had eaten half of the refreshments meant for the geezers.

"The team will be here," Auntie said, parking the car parallel to the mural-painted wall.

"Are you sure we won't get in trouble?" Dorothy asked, looking nervously up at Eva's gaping mouth.

"Trouble?" Auntie laughed. "Trouble is my middle name."

"Trouble is Grandma's middle name," Dorothy grumbled.

"Awe, come on, Dorothy," Grandma said. "Quit being such a stick in the mud. We aren't going to get caught. Nobody's expecting a bunch of old ladies to break into a roller rink to practice roller derby."

Dorothy could have sworn she felt the ground shake a little. "But why can't you practice somewhere else?"

"Like where?" Grandma said. "Look, hon. We've got less than two days to get these old girls back into derby shape, and I haven't found a single senior center that would give us the green light to roll. 'Against our policy,' they said. 'You'll break a hip,' they said." Grandma huffed. "Well, they can all just kiss my big, ol' saggy…"

"Easy now," Auntie warned.

"Big, ol' saggy skate bag," Grandma said. "What'd you think I was going to say, Venom?"

Dorothy scratched the back of her neck. She had thought the geezer bout was a great idea and was sure it would make enough money to save the building, but she was beginning to have a very bad feeling about this.

Auntie shut off her headlights and they sat in the car in dark silence.

Dorothy looked up at the mural. Eva's face seemed even more menacing in the dark. The black, missing space where her mouth had once been seemed larger. Hungrier. Dorothy decided to watch the parking lot instead. Hopefully the geezers wouldn't show. It seemed strange that there wasn't even one player there yet.

Ten minutes passed by. Grandma finished off the tray of crab puffs and then laid the seat back to rest her eyes. Within seconds she was snoring like a dragon with a sinus infection.

Dorothy tapped Auntie on the shoulder. "Can we go now? It's been like a year."

"Hush now," Auntie said. "They'll show."

Just then, a white bus squealed around the corner and into the parking lot. It bounced through the field of potholes, its headlights nearly blinding Dorothy, and screeched to a stop right next to Auntie's car. Music pulsated from inside the bus. It was so loud that it made Dorothy's teeth rattle. The decal on the side of the bus read: Rainbow Ranch, An Active Senior Living Facility.

Grandma startled awake. "It wasn't me, Officer," she said, waving her arms in front of her face.

"Wake up, Shotgun," Auntie said. "It's just the raisin mobile. The geezers are here."

Like on a spaceship, a large door on the side of the bus hissed open and a ramp slid forward. The music was so loud now that it could wake the dead. A pale, wrinkled woman with a hunched back appeared at the top of the ramp opening and belted into a hand-held intercom, "I'm a gangsta granny and I'm here to say, if you see me rollin', just get outta my way. Hurty Gerty's the name, playin' derby's my gas. Don't like how I roll? You can kiss my…"

"Gerty!" Auntie called, quickly getting out of the Malibu. "We've got a child here," she said, gesturing to Dorothy.

Dorothy ducked low and peeked out at Gerty from over her door.

Gerty tossed the handset over her shoulder and hopped easily from the ramp to the ground.

"Venom! My home girl!" Gerty said once the music had stopped. She pushed up the sleeve on her housecoat and punched Venom hard in the shoulder.

126

Auntie laughed, cracked her knuckles, and punched the old woman back.

"Come on, Dorothy," Grandma said, reaching for her skate bag. "You can't tell me you're afraid of a bunch of little old ladies."

"Not afraid," Dorothy lied. "I'm just, uh, really sleepy all of a sudden." She reached for a floor mat and draped it over her shoulders like a blanket. "Good night! Have a great practice, Grandma."

"Aw, come on, Dot," Grandma said. "I want to introduce you to my old teammates. You'll like the Geezer—er, Galactic Gals. They don't bite. Much."

After several minutes of prods and threats, Grandma finally dragged Dorothy out of the car and into the middle of the pack of old ladies. Dorothy did her best to keep behind Grandma's skate bag. There had to be twenty or thirty crazy old ladies in all. By appearance, none of them seemed more dangerous than those cookie-making grannies on TV commercials, but she wasn't taking any chances.

"For the fund-raiser bout, we've split into two teams," Auntie said.

Grandma raised a fist in the air. "Let me hear it for the Whippity Snaptters!"

Half of the old women cheered and whistled.

"Now let's make some noise for my team, the Auntie Establishment!" Auntie said.

The other half of the women clapped and whooped.

"Dorothy," Grandma said, pushing her granddaughter forward, "let me introduce you to my team."

Grandma gestured to the petite rapper. "You already know Hurty Gerty."

"'Sup." Gerty bumped her chest with her fist, and Dorothy wasn't sure if that was a greeting or if the old lady had indigestion.

Grandma reached up and patted the shoulder of a very tall, broad-shouldered woman with auburn hair. "This here is Bigfoot."

Dorothy could have sworn Bigfoot's hair slid forward an inch when the woman nodded hello.

"Bigfoot is an impassable blocker," Grandma said. "She's also BangBang's big sister. Where is Brenda anyway?" Grandma asked, scanning the group.

"Probably just running late," Bigfoot said in a quiet, deep voice.

"Not likely," Auntie said under her breath.

"Have a little faith, Venom!" Grandma said.

Auntie propped a fist on her hip and shook her head. "Honey, I lost my faith thirty years ago."

Grandma ignored Auntie and continued to introduce her team. There was a chubby, pale woman with white hair named Marsha Mellow; Polly Dartin', a top-heavy blond in a pink cowboy hat; Frieda Livery, a petite dark-haired woman wearing a Gino's Pizza jacket; and Hot Flash Phyllis, a gray-haired biker chick in head-to-toe leather. Other team members included Connie the Cougar, a curvaceous orange-haired woman in tight-fitting cheetah print, and a heavy woman with dark brown skin and bright-blue curls named OffHer Rocker Rosie. Rosie was riding an electric wheelchair scooter with a bumper sticker that said, "My other wheels are roller skates."

After the first six or so introductions, Dorothy started to lose track of who was who. And Auntie still had to introduce her team, the Auntie Establishment.

Vanessa pointed out women as she rattled off skate names: Auntie Anxiety, Auntie Maim, Auntie Dote, Auntie Acid, Auntie Fungal, Auntie Freeze, Auntie Matter, Auntie Septic, Auntie Wrinkle Cream, Auntie Virus, Auntie Inflammatory... Before long, they were just a blur of old lady faces to Dorothy. Good thing they were all Aunties. She'd never remember so many skate names.

As the women stepped forward for introductions, Dorothy couldn't help but notice that most of them were in pretty poor shape. It was hard to imagine any of these women having ever played professional roller derby. One Auntie was hunched over a walker; a couple other players were leaning on canes; and OffHer Rocker hadn't left her electric scooter since being lowered down on the bus ramp. Dorothy wasn't sure if the big woman could even walk. How in the world were these old ladies going to skate? Or bout? In two days? Dorothy bit the corners of her lips, which were beginning to feel itchy. Maybe it was the Wet n Wild strawberry lip balm she'd used that Grandma gave her out of her old skate bag. This geezer bout seemed like a worse idea every minute.

When Venom had finished, Gerty yelled, "Enough with the intros, yo! Let's play some *roller derby!*"

Suddenly, the parking lot trembled. A crack formed at the base of the wall and ripped up the side of the mural, creating a jagged gap between Eva and the other two skaters.

"What the…?" Auntie asked.

"*Back away from the building!*" Grandma yelled, sheltering Dorothy with her body.

The flock of old ladies scuttled backward, but as quickly as the shaking started, it stopped again and everything was calm.

"Calm down, everyone!" Grandma said, squeezing Dorothy's hand. "Nothing to worry about. Probably just shifting soils. Happens all the time around here. How about we all go in? It'll be safer inside."

Safer? Dorothy thought, looking up at Eva. If anything, Eva was more dangerous under Galactic Skate's roof.

The old ladies filed past Grandma and Dorothy and around the corner to the back entrance of the building. Dorothy could have sworn Eva's gaping hole of a mouth was silently laughing.

After all the women were out of sight, Grandma spanked Eva's painted bottom with her leopard-print skate bag. "Behave now, Eva!"

The wall creaked in reply, and a chunk of brick popped loose, flying past Dorothy and missing her by less than an inch.

"Hey!" Dorothy squealed.

"Nothing to see here," Grandma said, quickly scooping up the fallen bit of wall and stuffing it into her bag. It looked like Grandma has something shiny in her hands, but Dorothy couldn't tell. Grandma hooked the bag over her shoulder. "Whole darn place is falling apart."

Chapter 16

"What in the world happened here?" Auntie Venom asked after the back door clanked shut behind the geezers. Dorothy found the light switch and fluorescent bulbs buzzed to life, as well as a few rickety ceiling fans.

"Looks like a bomb went off," Hot Flash Phyllis said as they crossed the burned carpet and entered the skate floor.

The bleachers had been removed, but otherwise nothing had changed. The cracked and half-naked mirror ball was still embedded in the center of the skate floor, surrounded by yellow tape and a thousand shards of broken glass, glimmering like wicked little teeth in the dim light.

Polly Dartin' waved her pink cowboy hat in front of her face. "Phew-wee! You really ticked off ol' Eva this time, Sally."

"Sally was always ticking Eva off," Gerty said.

"Let's just get the glass off the floor and focus on skating, girls," Grandma said.

She went to get a broom and turn on some music as the old women laid aside their canes and orthopedic shoes and strapped on roller skates.

Dorothy could hardly bring herself to watch as the old women wobbled to their feet and skated out onto the rink. It was like watching thirty baby wildebeests learning to walk for the first time.

"Gear check!" Auntie ordered.

Dorothy scurried to get out of the way as the old ladies lined up in front of Venom. Some of them seemed to be getting the hang of their skates again, but most of them looked like they had about as much control of their bodies as a pack of roller-skating zombies. What if someone broke a hip? Or worse? The thought made Dorothy's whole body itch.

Auntie rolled back and forth in front of the women like a drill sergeant surveying her troops. "Where are all your mouth guards and helmets, ladies?" she barked.

"Can't I just take out my teeth?" one of the Aunties asked, spitting dentures into her hand.

"Helmets? Are you serious?" OffHer Rocker Rosie said. Her ankles were buckling inward from her massive weight. "I had my hair did today. I'm not messing this up," she said, fluffing her bright-blue curls.

"So you want to crack your head like an egg?" Auntie Venom asked, her nose an inch away from Rosie's.

OffHer Rocker huffed. "Never happened before."

"Except to Eva Disaster," Polly Dartin' said, biting her lip.

Connie the Cougar tapped a long fingernail on the center of Polly's chest. "I thought her heart gave out."

Bigfoot shook her head, making her auburn hair slip backward on her scalp. "It wasn't her heart. It was her head."

"It was gangsters." Gerty pointed her fingers like guns and shot off a round of invisible bullets.

"Gerty! You think everything is gangsters," Marsha Mellow said.

"Didn't her front wheels pop off?" one of the Aunties asked. "They never found those wheels, did they? Gold wheels, remember?"

Just then music started pumping in through the big speakers.

"That's enough Eva talk," Auntie Venom said in a hushed tone. "Sally's spent thirty years trying to forget about that night. Now don't you go reminding her."

"Reminding me of what?" Grandma asked, entering the floor with a push broom in one hand and a box of old helmets in the other.

"How it feels to get your butt kicked," Auntie howled.

Grandma cackled. "Bring it!"

Chapter 17

Thirty minutes later...

Chapter 18

The following day was Thanksgiving. Auntie Venom came over early to heat up the oil to fry the turkey. Sam helped Auntie in the kitchen while Dorothy helped Grandma decorate the house with a funky collection of Christmas decorations, most of which Grandma had made herself. Zombie snowmen, skeletal Santa Clauses, and coffin-shaped Christmas lights were strung on a black Christmas tree.

Dorothy could hear Sam gushing about Jim Schwartz in the kitchen. "Jim ordered me a Shirley Temple!" she exclaimed. "Jim let me have two desserts!" Jim this, Jim that. It was never ending. Dorothy did everything in her power to tune Sam out.

When they were done decorating, Grandma's funeral-home apartment looked even spookier than before, which was really saying something.

Mom and Jim Schwartz arrived right at four o'clock. Dorothy gulped nervously when the doorbell rang. Her plan was to act super cool, but her voice was quivering as she said hello and reached out to shake Jim's hand. Instead, he wrapped his long, boa constrictor arms around her and nearly squeezed the life right out of her. Jim was freakishly tall with broad shoulders and an even broader smile. He towered over Mom and looked like a giant next to Sam. He wore a suede jacket, a cowboy hat, and dark jeans ironed into sharp creases.

Dinner wasn't ready yet. The turkey fryer wasn't working, so Auntie was whipping up a sausage, crab, and turkey jambalaya instead.

Dorothy and Sam gave Jim a tour of the funeral home while the others finished making dinner and setting the table. Jim did his best to engage Dorothy in small talk. He asked about school, favorite subjects, and the kind of music she listened to. Dorothy tried to be polite and answered all his questions, but something about Jim made her skin crawl. Maybe it was the way he never stopped smiling; maybe it was the way he looked at her mom like she was a juicy cheeseburger; maybe it was the babyish gifts he had brought: a pink teddy bear for Sam and a Poopsy Loopsy doll for Dorothy.

Sam loved Jim, of course, and followed him around like a loyal puppy dog. It made Dorothy feel even more resentful. Mom's relationships never lasted more than a few months. To Dorothy, Jim was just another potential daddy that Sam would fall totally in love with, only to see him disappear forever after the breakup in a month or two.

After dinner, Dorothy helped Auntie clean up the kitchen before she bid them all good night. The jambalaya had been amazing, and Dorothy was full and happy.

Grandma, Sam, and Mom were in the living room listening to Jim play "Silent Night" on the guitar. Dorothy had to admit that Jim was a talented musician. But that didn't mean she liked him any better.

"Can you play us one of your songs, Mom?" Sam asked.

Dorothy took a seat next to Sam. "Yeah, I bet you have some great ones, Mom." She knew she sounded sarcastic, but how could she help it? Mom's voice was really pretty, but Dorothy always considered her more of a shower singer, not a country star.

"Okeydokey. If you insist, pardner." Mom's accent was as new as the guitar Jim sat in her lap. Mom pulled the guitar strap over her head and ran her fingernails down the metal strings. "I call this one 'Shotgun Mama.'"

Grandma's shoulders stiffened slightly, but no one but Dorothy seemed to notice.

Mom knocked her knuckles on the front of the guitar. "And a one and a two, and a one, two, three, four."

Well, Shotgun Mama did some dirty deals.
She kilt her rival, snatched the golden
wheels.
Shotgun Mama's got a smoking gun.
Roll on, Mama, I know what you done.
The key is in the coffin.
The clue is in the lid.

143

Someday they're gonna find it,
And you'll pay for what you did.
So roll on, Mama, roll on along,
Running from the law while I sing this song.
You think you're pretty tricky, you think you're pretty brave,
But my song is like a shovel and it's diggin' up your grave.
Yodalay, yodalay-hee-hoo! Diggety-diggety peek-a-boo.
Yodalay, yodalay-hoo-wee…

Grandma was on her feet waving her hands. "All right, all right," she said. Her face was an ashy gray. "I think we get the drift, Dolly."

"It's Holly now," Mom corrected, handing the guitar back to Jim. "Holly Mackerel, country star."

Diggety-diggety peek-a-boo? Dorothy thought. Sure, the song was catchy, but not in a good way. Also, Mom never even played the guitar. She just hit it like a drum.

"Aw, Grandma!" Sam said, disappointed. "I wanna hear the rest!"

"Don't you worry, darlin'," Jim said, winking at Sam. "You'll be hearin' that song plenty on the radio."

Mom blushed. "You really think so, Jim?"

Jim's permanent smile stretched even wider as he pinched Mom's knee. "I know so, Holly."

Gross! thought Dorothy.

Later, after Mom and Jim had gone back to their hotel, Grandma reported she wasn't feeling well and headed to bed early with Morti. He'd eaten a good portion of leftover turkey and crab bits, and Dorothy knew he was brewing the kind of gas that could peel paint off the walls.

Better Grandma's room than mine, she thought.

It was only seven o'clock, so Dorothy flipped on the TV. *The Frightmare before Christmas* was on. The skeleton Santa Claus character was riding a casket sleigh pulled by three skeletal reindeer.

"That's so funny," Sam said, turning herself upside down on the church-pew couch. She always watched TV like that. "The sleigh is exactly like something Grandma would build."

Sam was right. Grandma had built most of the furniture in the house out of funeral home leftovers and new and gently used coffins.

145

The character waved to the townspeople from his open casket sleigh through the flipped-back coffin lid.

Dorothy went cold and her hands began to itch. "Sam? What do you think Mom meant by 'The key is in the coffin. The clue is in the lid'?"

"How am I supposed to know?" Sam said, looking quizzically at Dorothy from her upside-down position.

Dorothy's palms were really tingling now. "Do you remember the words to Mom's song?" she asked.

"Sure," Sam said, turning herself right-side up again. She cleared her throat and sang, "Shotgun Mama made some dirty dills. She killed a ripe elf and...stole some golfing weasels?"

"Wasn't that 'golden wheels'?" Dorothy asked.

Sam crossed her arms. "You want me to sing it or not?"

Dorothy shrugged and Sam continued, "Shotgun Mama's got a smoking gum. Roll on deodorant; don't put it on your bum."

"Now you're just making stuff up!" Dorothy said.

Sam giggled.

Dorothy giggled too. And she remembered the rest

of the song now. She sang, "The key is in the coffin. The clue is in the lid. Someday they're gonna find it, and you'll pay for what you did."

"You don't suppose Eva is buried in our graveyard, do you?" Dorothy asked, looking out the window. Moore Memorial Cemetery was right across the street from the funeral home.

Sam shrugged. "I dunno. Grandma says ours is the only graveyard in town. I don't know where else she'd be."

Dorothy rubbed her tingling palms together. A plan was forming in her head. A big plan. A crazy plan. And, she had to admit, a dangerous, fairly gross, and all-around stupid plan. But if it worked (and it could work), they would know if Grandma really was Eva's murderer.

"Hey, Sam," Dorothy said, pushing the off button on the TV remote, "do you know where Grandma keeps her shovel?"

Chapter 19

The night sky was clear and dotted with stars. It was cold but not freezing, and a yellow half-moon grinned down on the two dark figures as they crept across the dry funeral-home lawn. Dorothy couldn't blame the moon for laughing. She and Sam looked ridiculous. They had searched for ninja costumes in Grandma's Halloween box—but there just weren't any.

They'd settled on the only black outfits in the box: a witch costume and a gorilla suit. Sam called dibs on the witch outfit because she thought the pointy hat was "cute." The costume was Grandma-sized though, so Sam had to tuck the long skirt into her pajama bottoms so she wouldn't trip. It made her look like she was wearing a dirty diaper, but Dorothy wasn't saying anything. Sam was already in a bad mood because Dorothy had put her in charge of carrying the shovel.

Silent as ghosts, they approached the graveyard gate. It felt colder in the shadow of the cemetery, like the ironwork fence separated two worlds—the land of the living and that of the dead. Dorothy shuddered with fear. She examined the gate through the tiny eye holes in the gorilla mask, searching for some excuse to turn back.

"No lock," she said, her breath hot and wet inside the gorilla mask, making her sound like Darth Vader.

No chain either. The smell of rubber and old dust filled her nostrils, adding to the sick feeling in the pit of her stomach. And to make matters worse, her whole body felt itchy now. Dorothy pushed the gate, and it swung forward with a spooky, metallic creak.

Frappit, Dorothy thought. "Too easy." This was by far the most messed-up idea she had ever had. Even crazier than driving Grandma's hearse.

She swung the flashlight's yellow beam, illuminating a

grassy garden of tombstones. Crosses and pillars formed shadowy fence lines, and at the center of the graveyard, a gigantic stone angel stood guard. The angel's wings were spread wide, ready to take flight and defend her skeletal tenants, should anyone disturb their final resting places. The voice in Dorothy's head said, *Go back to the funeral home! Leave the dead alone!* But Dorothy knew she wouldn't be able to sleep, not until she found Eva's coffin and knew what was inside that lid.

"You coming?" Dorothy said to Sam, who had fallen behind.

"I'm coming," Sam replied. "But why do I have to carry the shovel? This thing is heavy."

"Because I need to focus on finding the grave."

"Fine," Sam said, dragging the shovel behind her. "But you have to do all the digging."

Dorothy shuddered. What if the body was still icky? Like, not all dry bones yet? Was thirty years long enough for a body to turn to ash and dust? Or did embalming preserve it like a human sausage? Dorothy was getting queasy just thinking about it, so she pushed the thought out of her mind and focused instead on looking for a grave marker that said "Eva."

Thirty minutes later, they still hadn't found a single sign of Eva's grave.

"Can we go now?" Sam asked. "Please?"

"Fine," Dorothy said. "We'll leave after we finish this section." She had ditched the gorilla mask about two rows back, but her face felt as hot and itchy as ever.

"Are you sure she's even buried here?" Sam whined. "This shovel is giving me blisters."

Just then they heard a howl. An eerie *"Eeeeeeve!"* The voice appeared to be emanating from the angel. Terrified, they looked in the direction of the noise and saw a black shadow appear from behind the statue. "Who dares disturb my final rest?" the voice bellowed. It was a low female voice, and definitely angry.

Dorothy let out a bloodcurdling shriek as the dark being leaped down from the statue's pedestal.

Both girls scrambled backward, and Dorothy slammed into Sam, causing them both to fall hard onto their bottoms. The marble slab beneath them was

151

engraved with roses and hummingbirds and felt as cold as death.

The dark figure drifted across the lawn like a living shadow. Sam let out a bloodcurdling scream. Dorothy would have too, but she was paralyzed, unable to move or scream or even breathe. She willed herself to lift the flashlight, but her trembling hand refused.

"Shall I guess who you are then?" said the dark figure, drawing closer to the sisters. "Shotgun Sally's grandchildren come to desecrate the grave of Eva Disaster?"

Dorothy's tongue couldn't move to respond. How did this shadowy creature know?

"Answer me!" the figure bellowed, so close now that if Dorothy could have reached out, she would have been able to touch the hem of the shadow's long, tattered cloak.

"We, we…weren't going to defecate it," Sam said. "We were just going to dig it up. See?" Sam held up the shovel.

"Digger of the dead!" the shadow shrieked, lunging toward Sam. "Surrender your shovel to me now!"

It was then that Dorothy's protective instincts kicked in. Freed from her paralysis, she snatched the shovel from her sister's hand and swung it high and hard. The shovel hit the shadow's shoulder with a deafening *Ba-WANG*. The creature howled miserably and crumpled to its knees. Dorothy rose to her full height and raised the shovel high above her head. After this blow, the creature would never bother her or her sister or anyone else again.

"Dorothy!" croaked the shadow. "Stop, hon. It's me, Grandma!"

"*Grandma?*" Sam squealed.

"Flashlight!" Dorothy ordered. She would not be fooled by this treacherous beast, but she also didn't want to crush Grandma like a bug if the thing was telling the truth.

Sam quickly found the light and shined it into the shadow's face.

The figure squinted painfully into the light.

Dorothy was puzzled. The features were Grandma's, but her hair and face were coal black.

"Shoe polish," Grandma groaned.

"Oh my gosh!" Dorothy said, dropping the shovel to the ground. "Grandma! Are you okay?"

"You got me good, hon," Grandma croaked, holding her shoulder. "Way to kick your old granny's saggy butt." Grandma sat up, wincing as she held her left arm.

"Did…did I break you?" Dorothy asked.

"No, Dot. I don't think so," Grandma said. "But this is gonna make one monster of a bruise." At that Grandma grinned. "I can't wait to show the other geezers!"

"But how did you know we were here?" Sam asked, helping Grandma to her feet.

"Hon, I promised your mom I'd take care of you. You don't think you can sneak out of the funeral home without me knowing, do you?" Grandma said. "And besides, Morti scratched my door and woke me up just as you were sneaking out. Good thing too. He was gonna kill me with that turkey gas. Morti's back end is a weapon of mass disaster."

154

Betrayed by the stinking dog, Dorothy thought. "But why did you let us stay out here for so long?"

"You won't do it again now, will you?"

Dorothy and Sam shook their heads. Definitely not. This whole experience had been miserable.

"But weren't you worried that we'd find the grave and dig it up before you stopped us?"

"Nope. Eva isn't buried here, hon. In fact, she's not buried anywhere. Last I heard, she was sitting in an urn on top of her aunt Racine's television set."

"Cremated?" Dorothy said.

Grandma nodded.

"Then what did Mom mean by 'The clue is hidden in the coffin lid'?"

Grandma shrugged her shoulders and then flinched with pain. "Look, how the dickens am I supposed to know?" she replied, perturbed. "Your mom's an artist, and you know how they are. Always making up crazy stuff that nobody can understand. Anyway, I don't much appreciate being a suspect in a murder investigation, and I'm not sure I'd survive teaching you another lesson. So I don't want to hear about this anymore, girls. Got it?"

Dorothy and Sam nodded.

"Now help me get back to the house. This shoe polish is starting to crack, and I gotta get some ice on my shoulder."

The threesome walked back to the funeral home, Sam still dragging the shovel behind her.

Grandma tussled Sam's hair. "Digger O'Dead," she said with a chuckle. "You know Sam, that's not a half-bad skate name."

Sam giggled and repeated the name. "Digger O'Dead. I like it!"

At least someone got something out of this, Dorothy thought. *All I got was a rash and a dead end.*

Still, Mom's song must have meant something. Dorothy was sure of it. But if the clue wasn't in Eva's coffin, where was it?

Chapter 20

Dorothy trudged up the stairs, peeled off the gorilla costume, and went to her wardrobe to get her pajamas.

"Stupid, creepy closet," she said, slamming the door shut. Dorothy was sick of Grandma's house. Her nerves were officially shot, and all the crazy furniture made from leftover dead-people stuff was getting to her. The wardrobe had to be the worst. It had belonged to Dorothy's mom when she was a girl, and yeah, it looked fairly normal if you didn't examine it closely, but it was actually made out of two upright coffins joined together in the middle. For several nights after Dorothy moved in, she had woken up drenched in sweat. She had dreams that the Count and Mrs. Dracula were bickering over which one would get to come out of that thing and suck her blood dry.

Dorothy sighed and lay down on her bed. It was always something with Grandma. *Really, what kind of crazy person makes a closet out of a coffin?*

Dorothy jumped to her feet. "Coffin?" Was it possible that the clue to Eva's death had been right here in her bedroom the whole time?

Quick as a beetle, Dorothy scrambled to the hall bathroom, sat on the toilet lid, waited a whole minute, flushed, ran the sink for the count of six, and returned to her room—with a metal nail file.

Noiselessly, she opened the right door of her wardrobe. She ran her hand down the smooth, pillowed satin that lined the lid. No bumps, nothing unusual. Everything seemed totally normal. Normal for a coffin lid anyway. Then she tried the left door. About midway up, she felt something. A spot behind the satin where the pillowy batting sunk in, like there was a hollow spot behind the fabric.

Carefully Dorothy eased the point of the nail file into the glossy fabric. It cut easily, and she was careful not to create a hole any larger than her hand could fit through. Heart racing, she slipped her fingers into the fabric. She pushed the cottony filler aside, and there it was—a hole. She took a breath and pushed her hand inside. With the tips of her fingers she felt a tiny shelf.

She worked her hand in farther and touched something hard, cold, and metallic with spinning round things on either end. Her heart skipped a beat. She knew exactly what this was. And if the color was what she guessed it would be, it would prove something about Grandma she wasn't sure she wanted to know. But she had to know.

Slowly, she pulled the object out of the hole and through the fabric. Sitting in her shaking hand was the miserable truth: a broken roller-skate truck attached to a pair of golden wheels. Eva's wheels.

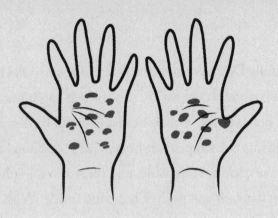

Chapter 21

Auntie Venom arrived at Grandma's house two hours before the geezer bout. They had planned to meet the rest of the players at the Yak 'n' Yeti Indian restaurant for a pre-bout lunch buffet, but Grandma was in a tizzy, unable to find an outfit that matched her arm sling. Her arm was so bruised and swollen that she had reluctantly resigned herself to coaching from the sidelines instead of playing in the game herself.

Dorothy felt bad about Grandma's injury, but now that she was sure Grandma was a killer, she thought she deserved to be hit with a shovel or worse. She also couldn't understand why Grandma cared so much about what she wore to the bout. Alex's dad, Jerry, had designed uniforms for all the old ladies, including Grandma. Dorothy imagined the uniforms would be frilly and covered in sparkly sequins, just like the outfits Jerry had designed for Alex's artistic roller-skating competitions. Dorothy couldn't wait to see Grandma and the other old ladies in outfits like that.

After an hour of waiting for Grandma to decide on something to wear, Auntie suggested they just heat up the leftover turkey jambalaya instead of driving to the Yeti. Fine by Dorothy. She had never tried Indian food, but the pictures made it look less than delicious.

Grandma finally appeared from her bedroom wearing a pink cheetah-print blouse with her sling painted to match.

She polished off the jambalaya, and they all piled into Auntie's Malibu and drove to the Thriller Auditorium. The Thriller was a worn-down concert auditorium that hosted rock-and-roll concerts and adult roller derby games.

Dorothy and Sam pressed their noses to the foggy

back windows and watched the snow fall. The cityscape was being blanketed in clean white. The snow reminded Dorothy of a powdered doughnut, which made her tummy feel warm inside, like everything might finally be working out. The Thriller wasn't haunted by Eva, and even if the geezers didn't skate well, they'd still make a lot of money from the ticket sales. Saving Galactic Skate was the only thing in her life that Dorothy was really excited about.

Grandma turned and smiled at Dorothy and Sam. "If all goes well tonight, we should have Galactic Skate up and running in a couple weeks!"

"Goody!" Sam said, clapping her hands together. "I can't wait to skate indoors again."

"Me too," Dorothy said. She had been burning to get back to skating, and the unpredictable and cold weather was making that nearly impossible.

"Now don't you girls go and get too excited about this," Auntie said, looking at them in her rearview mirror. "Last I checked, we only had thirteen tickets sold. Who all did you get to do the advertising anyway, Sally?"

"BangBang Brenda," Grandma said. "She used to run

162

all our derby promotions back in the day. Did a real nice job too."

"BangBang?" Auntie sucked air through her teeth. "Lord help us. She wasn't even at the practice, Sally. You know she's been forgetful lately."

"Because she's old?" Sam asked.

Auntie shook her head. "No, honey, it's not her age. It's her gambling. She goes up to that blasted Bucking Bronco Casino, and she doesn't come out. Loses all track of time."

Grandma stared at Auntie, a confused look on her face. "But I thought she quit gambling. I was sure of it."

"She did. But then she started dating Moochie Bretto." Auntie sighed. "And you know how Moochie is."

Moochie? Dorothy thought. *Like from the photo?*

"Don't remind me," Grandma said.

Dorothy looked down at her hands. Little red welts had begun to form on her palms. *Not again!* She willed herself to breath very slowly. "So…we'll still make some money tonight though, right?"

"Oh, honey," Grandma said, a concerned look passing

over her brow. "Don't you worry about anything, okay? We got a real good deal on the Thriller. And I'm sure BangBang will bring in the ticket sales. She knows how important this is."

"Oh, okay," Dorothy said. But her hands were really itchy. She closed her eyes and sat on her hands so she wouldn't scratch them. *Not the curse. Not now!* Surely Eva couldn't follow them to the Thriller. She was bound to Galactic Skate, right? Or was just Dorothy herself cursed?

When they arrived at the Thriller Auditorium, Auntie parallel parked behind the white geezer bus just as the bus door hissed opened.

OffHer Rocker Rosie's scooter exited the ramp. Once on the ground, Rosie launched the scooter into high gear, almost running Dorothy over. "Outta my way!" she barked. "Smells like someone lit a stink bomb in there."

"Sorry!" Polly Dartin' drawled, waving her pink hat in front of her nose as she exited the raisin mobile. "I forgot about all the cream in those Indian dishes. Y'all know I'm lactose intolerant."

"She's a real gas!" one of the Aunties joked.

Hurty Gerty slapped Polly on her back. "I guess we're going to have to change your name to Polly Fartin', eh?" Hurty Gerty's laugh sounded like a seal with a sore throat.

"Come on, girls," Grandma said, waving the team toward the front entrance. "Save the smack-talking for the rink."

The sign over the Thriller's main entrance read:

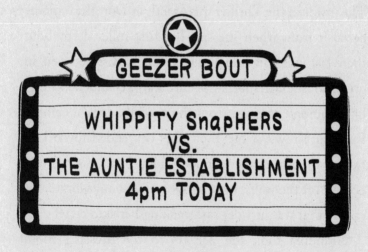

GEEZER BOUT

WHIPPITY SnapHERS
VS.
THE AUNTIE ESTABLISHMENT
4pm TODAY

Chapter 22

The inside of the Thriller was exactly as Dorothy remembered it from when she saw her first roller derby bout there last year. Big and grand, it was a cross between an opera house and a sports stadium. Large chandeliers hung like diamond earrings from the soaring, domed ceiling. Rows and rows of bleacher seats descended toward an expansive, oval-shaped wooden floor. Loud disco music echoed off the walls, making Dorothy's body vibrate. Or maybe that was just her rash making her skin crawl.

Grandma took the geezers to the dressing room while Dorothy and Sam went to find their team. The bleachers were all but empty, so it wasn't hard to spot the Slugs 'n' Hisses down in the front row, waving signs that read: Whip the SnapHers, I'm Anti-Auntie, and Geezers Rule!

Dinah was waving a giant poster drawing of an alien kitty cat riding a three-headed giraffe with the slogan "They're Coming!"

About ten rows above the Slugs, Alex and her two dads, Jerry and David, were drinking fancy coffees, chatting, and laughing comfortably.

It was such a nice picture of family togetherness that Dorothy almost wished her mom was there. But of course Mom hated roller derby, especially where Grandma was concerned. And she would have brought her smiley-faced boyfriend, Jim. Not exactly Dorothy's idea of a happy family gathering.

Sam tugged at Dorothy's arm. "Where are Vicious and Jade?"

"I don't know," Dorothy said, just noticing that they weren't with the rest of the team. Both girls had been invited, even though Dorothy hoped Jade wouldn't come. To say Jade had been acting strange lately was an understatement. Was she really trying to help the team, or was she trying to destroy it?

"We're over here," called a familiar voice.

"Speak of the devil," Dorothy said. She turned and saw Jade waving from her seat at a refreshment table next to the ticket booth in the lobby. Gigi was with her.

The table was covered with juice pouches and baggies filled with teddy bear–shaped graham crackers.

"What's this?" Sam asked, picking up a bag.

Gigi made a sour face. "Jade said she was going to bake cupcakes to make up for trying to burn Galactic Skate to the ground."

Jade perked up the collar of her jean jacket—it had been dyed black, probably to hide the burn marks—and made a sour face. "That fire was an accident. And I would have made cupcakes if my mom would have let me turn on the oven. This is the best I could do."

"Seriously, Jade? Your mom wouldn't let you turn on the oven?" Gigi's hands were on her hips. "Your excuses are getting crazier all the time. Are you sure you aren't just trying to ruin our fund-raisers?"

Jade opened and shut her mouth like a fish. "I'm here, aren't I?"

So far so bad, Dorothy thought, trying to breathe through her nerves. "It's okay, Gigi. Let's give her a break. You know how controlling Jade's mom can be."

Gigi threw her hands in the air. "Then why did she let Jade come to this thing?"

Jade pushed back from the table and narrowed her eyes at Gigi. "My mom said she had an important business meeting at the house tonight, okay? So she let me come." Her voice turned distant. "It was kind of weird, actually. Like she really wanted me gone."

"I want you gone," Gigi muttered.

Jade's shoulder's sagged, and she turned to look out toward the front entrance.

"Don't be sad!" Sam said, coming around to the other side of the table and wrapping her arms around Jade's shoulders. "I'm glad you're here. Us jammers have to stick together."

Jade's face softened for a second but quickly turned hard again, and she peeled Sam off her.

Sam looked hurt, so Dorothy bought five bags of teddy bears and sent her down to the bleachers to share them with the other Slugs.

Dorothy then pulled up a folding chair and sat in awkward, nervous silence between Jade, who was scribbling furiously in her sketchbook, and Gigi, who was watching funny MeTube videos on her cell phone. Twenty minutes passed, but only a trickle of people came inside to buy tickets. They all seemed to be Black Friday Christmas shoppers who had wandered by and were curious to see old ladies on roller skates.

Dorothy grew more nervous with every passing minute. She knew the ticket sales had to be miserable. All she wanted to do now was take her mind off the stress. She was feeling itchier by the moment and knew she'd feel better if Jade would just let her see what she was

170

drawing or Gigi would show her a funny video. But no one was sharing anything.

Shortly before four p.m., the lights in the hall dimmed. There was no way they had sold enough tickets to save Galactic Skate. Dorothy stood and was going to sit with the Slugs when she heard a loud male voice yelling, "I'm not paying for a ticket. I'm security, you hear? You should be payin' me!"

Dorothy cranked her head around the corner to see who was causing the trouble. Standing at the ticket window was an older couple—a petite woman with dark hair and darker sunglasses and a big man with a pile of gold chains draped around his neck. Dorothy recognized the big guy immediately.

"Calm down, Moochie," the woman was saying. She lifted her dark glasses to reveal bloodshot eyes rimmed in heavy mascara. "I'm one of the geezers," she said into the ticket window, "BangBang Brenda. Be a love and check the list."

The ticket guy confirmed Brenda's name, and she rounded the corner and sashayed right for the refreshment table with Moochie at her heels. Dorothy scrambled back to her seat. BangBang looked like a tiny doll compared to Moochie's hulking mass.

Moochie surveyed the juice boxes and crackers with disgust. "You call these refreshments?" he asked, his breath heavy with garlic. He placed a big sausage-y finger on one of the bags. "I'm a big guy, see? I can't live off little teddy bears." He leaned forward, and several crackers exploded under the pressure of his fat fingers. Moochie made a disappointed clicking sound with his tongue and picked up the bag of demolished teddy bears.

"Hmmmm. Too bad. How's about I do youse all a favor? I'll take these here busted ones off your hands, and I won't charge nothin' for my services."

"Okay," Jade said, holding out her hand. "That will be a dollar."

Moochie jerked his head hard to the left, and his neck made a loud cracking noise. He then unzipped the little bag and dumped the contents into his mouth.

"What crackers?" he said, spitting little bits of bear all over Jade, Dorothy, and Gigi.

Gigi was on her feet, fists balled and teeth barred.

Was she really going to try and beat up Moochie? That guy had to outweigh her by three hundred pounds!

"Aw, don't mind him," BangBang said gently, stepping in front of her boyfriend. She popped open her purse and presented Gigi with a dollar.

Moochie gave BangBang a hard look, his eyebrows angled into a bushy V shape.

"What?" BangBang said, returning his look. "I just won fifty-eight dollars at the craps tables. I can spare one buck for these girls, can't I?"

Moochie huffed and crossed his arms over his hairy, cracker-covered chest. BangBang seemed to have won this time.

"So you girls are with Sally's granddaughter's team?" BangBang asked. "The Slugs 'n' Hisses, right?"

"Uh, yeah," Dorothy said. "I'm Sally's granddaughter, Dorothy."

"So nice to meet you!" BangBang said, shaking Dorothy's hand vigorously. "You look just like Sally did when she was young. You remember Shotgun, don't-cha, Moochie?"

"I remember," grumbled Moochie. He plucked a teddy bear out of his chest hair, looked right at Dorothy, and snapped the bear's head in two between his teeth.

BangBang leaned in to get a better look at Dorothy's face. "You've got more freckles than Sally though. Those are freckles, aren't they?"

Dorothy nodded but knew BangBang was probably seeing rash spots. And the rash was about the last thing Dorothy wanted to talk about, so she changed the subject. "So, uh, my grandma said you did all the promotion for the geezer bout."

BangBang tilted her head like a bird. "Promotion? Oh snap!" she said, smacking her forehead. "Come on, Mooch! I gotta find Sally. I really messed up this time!"

Moochie waited until BangBang was several paces down the hall and then snagged three more bags of crackers. "Nice doin' business with youse," he said and then sauntered down the hall after BangBang.

"Let's get him!" Gigi said, flying out of her chair and rounding the table.

"Get him?" Dorothy said. "That guy is a wall of meat! You want to die over a bag of teddy bear crackers?"

Gigi spun around, hands on hips. "That was three bags!"

"Forget about it," Jade said, dejected. "Moochie can have them. We're not going to sell these anyway. The game is starting."

And so it was. The deep announcer's voice boomed over the loudspeaker, "Ladies and gentlemen, boys and girls! Let's hear a loud Thriller welcome for our first-ever geezer bout!"

Chapter 23

Dorothy rushed back to the bleachers and joined the team. Gigi sat next to her, but Jade was nowhere to be seen.

Dorothy cranked her head to the left and the right, and finally found Jade sitting several rows back with Alex and her dads. Jade was smiling and laughing like everything was just hunky-dory. No ruined fund-raisers, no soon-to-be-demolished Galactic Skate, no team falling apart and friendships being flushed down the toilet.

I don't get it, Dorothy thought. *I just don't get Jade.*

"First to the track," said the announcer, "coached by the legend, the one and only Shotgun Sally, please give a big Thriller welcome to the Whippity SnapHers!"

Grandma's team skated onto the floor, all wearing skintight, head-to-toe black faux leather bedazzled with silver studs. Grandma still had her pink sling on, but she had a whip in the other hand and was cracking it over her head like a crazed lion tamer. All the SnapHers were waving and blowing kisses and looking like they hadn't missed a single day on skates in thirty years.

Too bad more people aren't here to see this, Dorothy thought sadly. The geezers looked great.

BangBang was at the tail end of Grandma's group. She clearly looked upset and took only one look at the empty stadium seats before turning her eyes back to the rink.

Dorothy and her team were doing their best to make a lot of noise, but it barely put a dent in the silence.

"You ready to make some noise for the rival team?" the announcer asked.

There was a smattering of cheers.

"I can't hear you!" the announcer called.

Dorothy and the Slugs were on their feet screaming at the top of their lungs.

The announcer tapped his microphone. "Is this thing on?"

Unannounced, Auntie and her team skated out onto the floor, waving and whooping.

"Well, okay, here they are! Captain Auntie Venom and the Auntie Establishment!"

Auntie and her team were wearing headbands, round-rimmed sunglasses, and tie-dyed T-shirts that sported the slogan "Make Derby, Not War."

The loudspeaker made a scratching sound and they could hear the announcer asking, "And how about referees? Did any of them show up?"

Just then five guys in black-and-white jerseys skated out.

"Oh, here they are!" the announcer said. "We have uh…the Silver Mullet, Charlie Horse, Hal E. Tosis, Angel DelAmo, and Max Voltage." Angel spotted Dorothy and waved, mouthing, "Dude, look!"

Dorothy's heart skipped a beat. Max? She had no idea Max would be coming tonight. Angel either. But it was Max that made her heart thump madly inside her rib cage.

The refs skated around the perimeter of the rink. Dorothy stood to wave as they approached her side of the stadium, but she sat down again quickly and buried her head in her hands as Max passed by. She couldn't be sure, but she thought she was still covered in little red spots. How humiliating!

"And we can't forget our medics, Butch Casualty and Barry D'Alive. I'm sure these guys will have their hands full tonight."

There was then a pause while techno music rocked the stadium and laser lights bounced off the walls.

"All righty," said the announcer. "Let's do this thing!"

"This oughta be good," Gigi said. She held up her cell phone and set the video to record…

And with that, the game was over. Emergency response was called, and Barry D'Alive and Butch Casualty loaded Hurty Gerty onto a gurney.

Everyone exited the stadium and followed the gurney to the curb where Gerty was loaded into the back of an ambulance.

"You're gonna have a hard time competing with this bruise," Gerty said, pointing to her hip and laughing. "There's gonna be extra pudding for me back at the Raisin Ranch tonight, suckers!" she called as the ambulance doors were pulled shut.

Dorothy and all the geezers watched as Hurty Gerty was hauled away amid sirens and flashing lights.

"Well, that was fun," Grandma said unenthusiastically.

"How much did we make, Grandma?" Dorothy asked, afraid to hear the answer.

Grandma sighed. "Looks like we came in fifty dollars short of paying for the facility, hon."

"Here," Brenda said, opening her purse and handing Grandma a handful of bills. "I'm real sorry about this, Sally. I really am. How about you let me buy you a drink at Boogie Bingo down at the Rainbow Ranch? I won't even bring Moochie. I know you and him don't get along."

"Thanks but no thanks, BangBang," Grandma replied, her face as sad and saggy as a bulldog's.

Dorothy couldn't remember seeing Grandma so depressed. She was the kind of person who could laugh no matter what. She even laughed when she saw Dead Betty wrapped around the mailbox. She had also yelled and cried, pulled out some of her hair, and thrown her purse and both of her boots onto the roof of the funeral home. But this Grandma? This Grandma was checked out. Since when did Grandma turn down a party?

Regardless of what she had done in the past, Dorothy wanted to make Grandma happy again. Grandma had given her and Sam a place to live when they had no place else to go. She had taught them roller derby. And she was nice, in a throw-a-bottle-at-your-head sort of way. If Dorothy could find a way to get rid of Eva's curse and save Galactic Skate, she might be able to restore some happiness to this crazy little family of

183

hers. And she had to do it soon—before Jade or Mrs. Song or anyone else made Galactic Skate and the Slugs 'n' Hisses go away forever.

Chapter 24

The next morning…

Chapter 25

For a long time, Dorothy, Gigi, Jade, and Sam stood in the dark in front of Dinah's door and debated.

"You sure you want to do this séance thing?" Gigi said, dumping her fat pillowcase next to the gnome statue that held a sign that said "Welcome."

"Is a séance like a sleepover?" Sam asked. "I've never been to a sleepover."

"The sleepover is the cover, Sam," Jade said, tugging her black hand-knit hat down low over her ears.

"What's a cover?" Sam asked.

"Like a lie," Dorothy said, her stomach gurgling. Either this sneaky business was getting to her, or the crab cakes they'd had for dinner weren't settling well. "We don't want Grandma or anyone else to know that we're breaking into Galactic Skate."

"And summoning the ghost of Eva Disaster," Jade added. "Is someone going to knock or not? I'm getting cold."

"And wet," Dorothy said. The sky had started to spit cold drops of rain, and she could already feel her hair frizzing into clown mode.

"Fine. I'll do it," Gigi said, reaching for the door knocker shaped like a praying mantis head.

But before she could knock, the door flew open, revealing a heavyset man with light brown skin and long, dark, braided hair. "Ho, ho, ho!" he said in a deep, booming voice. He sounded exactly like Santa Claus. "Well, what do we have here? Let's see. I'll take three boxes of S'moresies, a box of Munchie Mints, and two tins of popcorn. You got any buttery ranch?"

"Uh…" Dorothy said. After all that time on the doorstep, they clearly had the wrong address.

"Stop kidding around, Dad!" called Dinah's voice

from somewhere inside the house. "Come on in, girl-friends! I'm in the living room."

The first thing Dorothy noticed as they passed through the entryway was the scent of burning sage. It smelled exactly like the smudge stick Jade had used, minus the burned carpet aroma. The house was pretty normal otherwise. An average-sized two-story with high ceilings, skylights, and tan carpet as far as the eye could see. The walls were decorated with an odd mix of artwork: Native American looking drawings, framed photographs of kittens in baskets, and an amateur landscape painting with Bigfoot peeking out from behind happy little trees.

Dinah was lying on her side in the middle of the living-room floor. Tendrils of white smoke rose from what looked like a rolled-up piece of newspaper sticking out of her ear.

"One more minute for your candle!" called a woman's voice from the kitchen.

"You're making a candle?" Sam asked.

"From earwax?" Jade added, gagging on the words as she said them.

"No, sillies," said Dinah. "I'm candling. It's a Hopi Indian thing. It gets all the gunk and bad spirits out of your head."

Just then, a timer dinged and Dinah pulled the tube out of her ear. "Wanna see?" She held the tube out for inspection.

Jade pulled off her hat and looked like she might throw up in it.

"Uh, maybe another time," Gigi said.

"Dinah, honey?" a voice called from the other room.

"Yeah, Mom?"

"I'm still packing my medicine pouch. Why don't you take your friends upstairs and show them your ET collection."

"Okay, Mom!"

"ET? Like the movie?" Gigi asked.

"You'll see."

Dinah led Dorothy, Gigi, Jade, and Sam up a staircase to a door with a yellow triangle-shaped sign that said "WARNING! Alien X-ing."

It was a small bedroom. In the center of the room was an unmade bed with star-patterned sheets. There was a neon-green rug in the shape of an alien head with two big, black eyes, and a solar system mobile hung from the ceiling-fan cord. All four walls were covered with shelves and shelves of little alien figurines: gray ones with big eyes; half-human, half-iguana creatures; slender white beings that looked like praying mantises; and blue aliens with an extra eyeball in the middle of their foreheads.

"You can put your stuff over there," Dinah said, pointing to a nightstand where a flying-saucer-shaped fishbowl sat. Inside the bowl, a chubby, orange goldfish was swimming lazily on its side.

"Nice fish," Dorothy said, dumping her pillowcase next to the table. She hoped the poor thing wouldn't die on them overnight.

"That's Lord Flushington," Dinah said. "He's more of a floater than a swimmer."

"I see that," Dorothy said.

"So, you really like aliens, huh?" Gigi asked, her eyes wandering around the room.

"Uh…" Dinah said, suddenly looking self-conscious. "Hey, can you guys keep a secret?"

Dorothy nodded. "Of course."

"Okay," Dinah said, her voice a whisper. "Brace your-selves. This may come as a really big surprise, but I am… an alien."

Jade laughed. "Okay, nice joke, Dinah." She took off her hat.

"No, I'm not kidding," Dinah said. "I mean, I'm not one hundred percent alien. I'm a hybrid."

And that's why Dinah is so weird, Dorothy thought. "So…does that make you psychic too?" she asked.

Dinah shrugged. "A little. I can try to read you if you give me a second." She placed one hand on her fore-head and held the other one out in Dorothy's direction. "Okay," Dinah said, "I'm seeing a polka-dotted crab,

Grandma Sally playing the drums, and skate wheels. Gold ones."

Dorothy's blood ran cold. She hadn't told anyone about the wheels. Not even Sam.

"So, how did I do?" Dinah asked, peeking out from under her hand.

"Uh, great, Dinah!" Gigi said with a big, fake smile. "Really, uh, neat."

"Cool!" Dinah said, clapping her hands together excitedly. "But you can't tell anybody about me being an alien. It's a secret. Even my dad doesn't know."

"That big dude downstairs?" asked Gigi. "That's your dad?"

"You girls ready to go?" called Dinah's mom from downstairs.

"*Woo-hoo!*" cheered Dinah. "Let's go catch that ghost!"

Chapter 26

Dinah's mom parked her white Jetta in Galactic Skate's weedy back parking lot. Big snowflakes were drifting to the ground and it was beginning to look a lot like Christmas, minus Santa, sugarplum fairies, and goodwill to all mankind. Dorothy shuddered, partly from the cold but mostly from the sinking feeling that this séance was a really bad idea.

"Ghost time!" announced Dinah, unlatching her seat belt and bounding out of the car like an eager puppy.

"Yippee!" Sam said, scrambling out after her.

The rest of the ghost hunters slowly exited the car and followed them.

"You do have that key now, don't you, Dorothy?" Dinah's mom asked, hooking her beaded, leather medicine pouch over her shoulder. She was wearing a turquoise jacket over a long, orange dress with a southwestern print. Dorothy had expected her to be really weird like Dinah, but Dinah's mom was actually pretty normal. She looked like Dinah—thin with crystal-blue eyes and mousy, brown hair. But where Dinah was all energy and enthusiasm, her mom was just sort of frazzled, like she'd tapped all her energy reserves several years ago and was now operating entirely on nerves and caffeine.

"I have the key right here, Mrs. Gibbs," Dorothy said, attempting to pull the shoestring necklace over her head. Unfortunately, Dorothy's hair was in full-frizz mode now, and she had to untie the shoelace just to get the key free.

"Where'd you get that?" Gigi asked.

"Grandma's skate bag," Dorothy said. She felt kind of bad about borrowing the key, but since Grandma had stolen it from Enzo in the first place, maybe it wasn't really a crime.

Dorothy inserted the old, silver key into the deadlock and turned. It clicked easily and the back entrance door creaked open on squeaky hinges. Dorothy peered into the dark. The only light came from the glow of the Hot Pizza sign.

"All clear," she whispered, her breath a puff of smoke in the chill of the skate hall.

Silent as mist, Mrs. Gibbs and the five girls slipped inside and locked the door behind themselves.

"Too dark," Gigi said, flipping a switch. A few fluorescent bulbs buzzed to life—one near Pops's rocket-shaped skate-rental desk, another over the snack-bar seating area, and a couple at the far end of the skate floor.

"That's enough light," Mrs. Gibbs said. "We don't want to scare our ghost away, now do we?"

"This is so cool!" Sam said, bouncing on her toes. "My first ghost hunt!"

"Take me to where Eva last made herself known," Mrs. Gibbs said, her voice taking on a low and mysterious air.

"That would be the skate floor," Jade said.

197

"Where she tried to squash us dead with a disco ball," Sam added, skipping ahead.

"Perfect," said Mrs. Gibbs. "We'll set up there."

The geezers had cleared the police tape and swept away the shattered glass two nights ago, but the broken disco ball was exactly where it had been since Halloween night, lodged securely in the wood floor.

From her leather medicine bag, Mrs. Gibbs produced a stubby red candle and a small box of wooden matches.

She struck a match and lit the candle in a single motion, letting the melting red wax drip like thick blood onto the top of the mirror ball. She secured the candle to the hot wax, bowed ceremoniously to the flame, and glided into a sitting position with the folds of her dress tucked neatly beneath her knees.

"Okay, girls," she said. "Everyone just sit on your pockets and close your eyes while I dial up Madame Trusso. She'll be able to contact Eva."

Sam sat to Dorothy's left, Gigi to her right, and Jade and Dinah on either side of Mrs. Gibbs, forming a tight circle around the broken mirror ball.

Mrs. Gibbs closed her eyes and swayed her hands to and fro above her head. "In through the nose and out through the mouth," she instructed in a calm voice, pulling in deep breaths as she spoke.

Dorothy closed her eyes but only counted three exhales before she chickened out and opened them again.

Mrs. Gibbs's face was calm and expressionless now. And she was wearing a gym sock on her right hand.

It was an old, yellowing sock adorned with button eyes, lopsided red felt lips, and a messy mop of black yarn for hair.

"OMG," Gigi whispered to Dorothy. "Do *not* tell me that Madame Trusso is a sock puppet."

"*Silence!*" shrieked the sock puppet.

Sam let out a high squeal, and Dorothy, Gigi, and Jade almost jumped out of their skin.

"Pay no attention to the sock," said the sock. It had an eerie voice, loud and raspy with a Russian accent. And what was spookier was that Mrs. Gibbs's lips were not moving. Not even a little.

"I am the great Madame Trusso! This puppet is but a vessel through which I am speaking to you now."

Gigi laughed nervously. "Right. Okay, Mrs. Gibbs. Nice one. Ha-ha. You got us."

The sock cocked its yarn-y head to one side. "Mrs. Gibbs isn't here right now."

"Dinah! Make your mom stop," Jade said. "She's freaking me out!"

Dinah didn't say anything. Her eyes were still closed, and she was rocking and humming quietly to herself.

"Jade Song-Mizirov wishes me to stop?" questioned the sock. "How is it that the child of the fearless Roman Mizirov is 'freaking out' just because of a cute, itty-bitty sock like me?"

Jade face turned as white as a sheet of paper. "How... how do you know my dad?" she asked.

The sock made a little shruggy gesture. "What can I say? He's dead, I'm dead. I've got the inside scoop on dead people."

"Well, you've got my attention," Gigi said.

"Excellent!" exclaimed Madame Trusso. "Shall we proceed with the séance?"

All the girls nodded, except for Dinah who was deep in la-la land.

"Oh goody," said the sock with a delighted cackle. "First things first. Have you brought an item connected to the deceased? A photograph or a lock of hair, perhaps?"

"Uh, no?" Dorothy scratched her itchy palms. "Do we need an item?"

"Fools!" cried the sock. "Without an item, how does the great Madame Trusso locate the correct frequency?"

Sam leaned over to Dorothy. "How about this?" she whispered, withdrawing a folded piece of paper from her back pocket. "I found it in one of Grandma's drawers."

At least I'm not the only one taking Grandma's stuff, Dorothy thought as she unfolded the paper.

"*Do your legs look like they belong in a zoo?*" Dorothy read aloud. "*Get rid of those gorilla gams with new Smooth as a Baby's Bottom hair-removal cream!*"

Sam pointed at the news clipping. "Other side."

201

"Ohhh," Dorothy said, flipping the fragile paper over. "*Eva D. Setsuko, a.k.a. Eva Disaster, died on Halloween night due to injuries sustained during a roller derby match at the town's local roller disco, Galactic Skate.*"

With an electric crackling sound, one of the fluorescent lights over Pops's desk went dead. The hair on Dorothy's neck stood on end.

"Go on!" demanded Madame Trusso.

The paper was now shaking in Dorothy's hands. "*Detectives suspect foul play and are offering a reward to anyone providing information leading to the whereabouts of a missing pair of gold roller-skate whee—*"

Just then, the puppet snatched the paper from Dorothy's hands and crumpled it in its sock mouth like it was chewing.

"Hey! I wasn't done reading that," Dorothy said, reaching for the paper. But it was too late. The puppet spat the brittle newsprint into the candle's flame, and it was gone in a puff of ash and smoke.

"*Excellent!*" cried Madam Trusso. "The frequency has been located." The sock began to sway back and

202

forth and mumble in some unrecognizable, ancient-sounding language.

The weird chanting stopped abruptly. "I sense great anger with this one," the sock warned. "I do not suggest we—"

The sock stopped speaking abruptly and fell limp and lifeless on Mrs. Gibbs's wrist.

"What's going on?" Gigi whispered.

Dorothy felt something cold whoosh past her, and the candle flame blew out.

Sam squealed.

Gigi grabbed Dorothy's knee. "What was that?"

Not again, Dorothy thought, her whole body trembling. "Dunno," she managed to say. "T-too dark."

After what felt like an eternity, her eyes began to adjust. And she immediately knew something was wrong with Jade. Jade's head was tilted back, jaw slack, mouth open, and her body was twitching. Without warning, Jade's head jerked forward and her eyes snapped open. But they were empty.

An unearthly voice gurgled up from Jade's throat.

"Who dares summon me?" it growled. "Who dares invoke the ghost of the fastest, the greatest, and the best?"

Jade's deadened gaze swung left and then right, and finally settled on Dorothy.

"*You?*" Jade howled, her nostrils flaring. Jade's body rocked forward, and she began pacing back and forth on her hands and knees like some kind of caged animal. "Tired of my little curse, are we? Come to beg my forgiveness, hmmmm?" Jade tossed her head back and let fly a spooky howl.

"Well, too bad, Sally! This is my home, my domain! Eva Disaster is still the fastest, the greatest, and the best. You took my life, you stole my wheels, but you will never take my place!"

Dorothy watched Jade in paralyzed terror. She willed herself to breathe and think of something—anything—to say. She had to get Eva to leave Jade, to leave them all alone, if she could. She knew it was only a matter of time before Eva actually killed someone. "I… We don't want to take your place. We just want to play roller derby here in peace. Honest!"

"*Lies!*" screamed Jade. Electric sparks rained down on them from the hole in the ceiling where the ball had once hung. "My curse shall remain until you admit your guilt and *give me back my wheels*! Until then, all who play roller derby here will face the wrath of Eva Disaster. Starting with you, Shotgun!"

Oh frap! Dorothy thought, scrambling backward. *This is the part where Eva rips my throat out and I join the ghost club.*

Of all the crazy ways Dorothy had imagined herself dying—devoured by flesh-eating jungle bacteria, lost in space, buried alive—this had to be worse than all of those things combined.

Just then, the sock puppet shook violently, like a flat-line patient being zapped back to life. Madame Trusso coughed up a gum-ball-sized hunk of lint and then screeched, "Eva! I command you to *leave this child*!"

Jade swung her head in Mrs. Gibbs's direction and roared like an angry tiger, her mouth a wide circle of noise and hate. The whole room was alive with crackling, electric energy now, and all the hairs on Dorothy's body were standing on end.

"I said, *leave her!*" the sock boomed.

Jade's roar transmuted into a squeal of pain. Her body suddenly became as still as a rock, and she tumbled backward.

Dorothy jumped to her feet and ran to her friend. "Jade! Jade, are you in there? Wake up!" she said, shaking Jade's limp shoulders. "She's not moving, not breathing," Dorothy screamed. Her heart was pounding violently inside her rib cage. "*Jade!*"

Suddenly, Jade's body lurched. She rolled onto her side, coughing and sputtering like a nearly drowned swimmer.

"What? What happened?" Jade said once she could speak again. "Did I pass out?"

Dorothy breathed a huge sigh of relief. "Thank God you're all right! You were… Eva, she, she…"

"Do not trouble yourself or Jade," Madame Trusso said gently. "Eva is gone now and will not return to this circle. I should advise you, however, that the wrath of this destructive one has been ignited."

"Uh, like, more than before?" Gigi said.

"Yessss," the sock hissed. "You have not seen the last

of Eva Disasterrrr." And with that, the sock dropped limp into Mrs. Gibbs's lap and was silent.

Mrs. Gibbs blinked a few times and smiled pleasantly. Her smile disappeared when she saw the look on Dorothy's face. "Oh dear!" she said. "You look so... upset. Did that naughty Madame Trusso scare you?"

Mrs. Gibbs returned the sock puppet to her medicine pouch and shook Dinah's knee gently.

Dinah yawned and stretched like a kitten just waking up. "That was the best tea party ever, Mr. Hatter," Dinah cooed. She blinked twice and seemed startled to see everyone staring at her. "Oops!" she said. "The séance, right? Did I miss anything? Did we start yet?"

Before anyone could respond, they heard a loud *smash-bang*. The front door of Galactic Skate had been kicked in.

"Police!" boomed a man's voice from the front of the building. "Hands where I can see them!"

Dorothy slowly raised her hands above her head, and the other girls followed suit.

A pair of chubby hands holding a gun appeared at the entrance to the skate floor.

"Don't shoot!" Dorothy called. "We're just kids!"

"Dorothy Moore?" The gun disappeared and Uncle Enzo came around the wall. "What the heck are you girls doing breaking into my building?" he asked. "We saw the light and thought it was thieves. Not that there's much to steal around here." Enzo looked back over his shoulder and called, "It's okay, Mrs. Song! All clear. Just those pesky derby girls."

"Derby?" said a woman's voice. "Blossom! Jade, honey? Are you here?"

Jade groaned and lay back down on the floor. "Here, Mom. Right here."

Chapter 27

The following day, Dorothy was miserable. She moped around her bedroom all morning, not wanting to eat and too anxious to nap, even though she was exhausted. She had only slept for a couple hours after the séance. Her brain kept chewing away on everything that had happened at Galactic Skate. They had been pretty lucky considering; Enzo didn't want to press charges, and Jade only had a little goose egg on the back of her head.

Still, Mrs. Song had been furious. She vowed to see Galactic Skate scraped, sold, and gone for good. And what was worse, Dorothy was starting to agree with Mrs. Song. Even worse, Mom called from Nashville on the night of the séance. Sam had blabbed about the evening's disaster and now Mom had renewed hate for roller derby. She forbade Dorothy from playing. As if. Mom had hardly even called or texted since she left after Thanksgiving.

It was clear now that Eva Disaster wanted them all dead. Was Galactic Skate worth dying for? Dorothy knew that losing it would break Grandma's heart—the crazy old lady loved Galactic Skate—but then again, maybe Grandma should have thought about that before she killed Eva in the first place. Murder over a stupid pair of golden wheels? The wheels weren't even made of real gold. Before hiding them back in the closet door, Dorothy had bit them just to make sure. She had nearly cracked her tooth on the wheel. Definitely not gold.

"Dorothy!" Grandma called, nearly making her jump out of her skin. "Get your booty-swingin' bottom down here."

"You're thinking of Gigi, Grandma!" Dorothy yelled back. Crazy, old killer Grandma.

"It will be when I'm done with it," Grandma returned.

"Who said you could invite all the Slugs 'n' Hisses over here for a dance party?"

Oh frap! Dorothy thought, leaping out of her bed and pulling on a skirt and loose-fitting T-shirt. She had totally forgotten about their talent-show rehearsal.

When she got to the kitchen, all the Slugs were there: Gigi, Alex, Dinah, Juana, Lizzy, Ruth, Dee, and even the Quints, zipping around Grandma's house in their roller skates. The only person missing was Jade, and she was probably grounded until she was as old as Grandma.

"For your information, G-ma, we are trying to save your stupid, haunted second home," Gigi was explaining. "You could be a little more grateful."

"Save it? With a hoodoo-voodoo dance?" Grandma said. "You kids are getting strange, even by my standards." She waved her good arm dismissively and headed back to her bedroom.

"It's not a voodoo dance, Grandma," Dorothy called. "We're competing in a talent show. If our dance wins, then all the ticket money goes to Galactic Skate."

211

"What?" Alex said. She was wearing a cute, pink-sequined jogging suit, and she looked angry. "What do you mean *if* we win, then we get the money?"

Gigi propped a fist on her hip. "Win against who? I thought we were just putting on a good show here, not competing."

"Yeah, I'm doing a psychic magic show," Dinah said.

"And I'm singing a song I wrote," Dee added.

Everyone stared at Dee, dumbfounded.

"I'm sorry," Dorothy said finally. She had been so busy with the geezer bout and the ghost problem that she had neglected to tell her team about the bet she had made with Priscilla. "The thing is, we kind of have to beat the Pom-poms in a dance contest to get the money. But it's really not a problem, is it? Because you're an amazing jam dancer," Dorothy said, pointing to Gigi. "And you're an amazing artistic roller skater," she said, pointing to Alex. "We'll have the best dance ever, won't we?"

Alex crossed her arms over her chest and shook her head. "You've really done it this time, Dorothy."

212

"Why? What did I do?" Dorothy said.

"The Pom-poms aren't just a club. They're a competitive cheerleading squad. They know how to dance. They also know how to do flips and tumbles and all sorts of things this team can't do."

"I can tumble," Ruth said, giggling at her own joke. Rolling Thunder was famous for her spectacular crashes.

Lizzy removed a calculator from her coat pocket and started punching buttons. "According to my calculations, our chance of success is approximately 7.695 out of one hundred."

"That sounds optimistic, Geekzilla," Gigi said. "We're skaters, not dancers."

Just then an idea hit Dorothy. "Hey, can you guys trust me?"

Gigi rolled her eyes. "Do we have a choice?"

"Woo-hoo, crazy Dorothy idea!" Dinah cheered.

Just then Grandma appeared from her bedroom wearing a hot-pink leotard, black-and-white zebra-striped leggings, and her pink cheetah-print arm sling. "Take your crazy ideas down to the basement, will ya?" she said.

"*Groovin' with the Geezers* is on in five minutes, and I don't want you all messing up my warm-up."

Grandma turned her back to the girls, bent forward, and touched her toes with her good hand.

Dorothy's team all made faces like they'd just been served a bowl of live worms for lunch. Half of them shielded their eyes. The back of Grandma's leotard was nothing more than thin, pink material and wedged between oversized butt cheeks.

"And a one and a two," Grandma said, starting in on a round of squats.

"Basement it is!" Dorothy announced.

After four hours of planning and practice, Dorothy had a good feeling that her idea would work. They would beat the Pom-poms at the talent show and save Galactic Skate with the money. After everything that had gone wrong in the last month, their luck was sure to change now, wasn't it?

Chapter 28

Over the next two hours...

WELCOME TO THE J. ELWAY ANNUAL COMMUNITY TALENT SHOW AND FUND-RAISER! ALL YOUR TICKET MONEY GOES TO CHARITY, SO REMEMBER TO VOTE. THE PERFORMANCE WITH THE MOST VOTES GETS TO PICK THE RECIPIENT.

Looks like mostly boys...

Who's wearing those top hats? Must be a magic act.

FIRST TO THE STAGE: DINAH GIBBS, PSYCHIC MAGICIAN!

Please choose a card.

I will now guess your ca

Your destiny is linked a loosened skate. The final bout will seal you fate. What happened before will happen agai Cure the curse or lose your friend.

I call Dorothy Moore to assist me!

You're freaking me out, Dinah.

So, was I right?

You really think so?

Bad for her, good for us.

Be nice, Vicious. You know what they say about karma.

AND FOR OUR NEXT ACT, THE SLUGS 'N' HISSES PERFORMING A DANCE TO "WHY CAN'T WE BE FRIENDS." WELL, THIS IS A SURPRISE. THE DANCE IS DEDICATED TO THE POM-POMS!

JAM DANCER GIGI AND ARTISTIC SKATER ALEX TAKE TURNS SHOWING OFF THEIR BEST MOVES WHILE THE REST OF THE SLUGS DANCE BACKUP.

WITH A SLIDE STEP SLIDE, CHANGE DIRECTION. SLIDE, STEP, SLIDE, FINGER SNAP. THE ROUTINE WAS GOING PERFECTLY UNTIL...

Chapter 29

Dorothy kicked off her skates and flew out of the auditorium. Wherever Priscilla was, she would find her and would make her pay for this.

Fortunately, Priscilla was easy to find. Dorothy stomped down the hall in her socks, tracking a trail of foam that led her from the auditorium to the girls' bathroom.

She placed an ear to the door. The only noise was the drone of a hand dryer. Priscilla had to be alone in there.

Dorothy kicked the door open with her soggy stocking foot, and Priscilla screamed and flattened herself against the far wall until she realized who it was.

"What do you want, Speed McQueen?" said Priscilla, refocused on blowing her hair back to gorgeous.

"I want our performance back, that's what. I want Galactic Skate back. I want my team back." Dorothy's voice dropped to a growl. "You've ruined everything now. Speeding up the music? Very funny. But loosening all the wheels on our skates? Not okay." Dorothy was nose to nose with Priscilla now. "What if one of us had fallen off the stage, hmm? What if one of us had gotten killed?"

Priscilla rose to her full height. "Excuse me?" she said, glaring down her nose at Dorothy. "If you haven't noticed, I've got my own problems to deal with right now. You must have wrecked your own show because we didn't do it. You're the clumsy one. You screw up everything, remember?"

Dorothy balled her hands into fists. "That's hilarious coming from someone who just set herself on fire!"

Priscilla cracked her knuckles. "Last straw, Dorothy!"

Just then, the bathroom door swung open. "There you are!" Gigi said, grabbing Dorothy by the arm and pulling her into the hallway. Gigi was out of breath. "The auditorium! There's something you have to see!"

Chapter 30

Gigi dragged Dorothy down the hallway and in through the back door of the auditorium.

It took a moment for Dorothy's eyes to adjust. The auditorium was black, but the stage was ablaze with spinning rainbow laser beams, strobe light flashes, and spotlights. Electronica rocked the room, bumping a base beat through Dorothy's entire being.

She squinted. "Is…is that…Merdusa?" Merdusa played for one of Dorothy's favorite senior roller derby teams, the Flatiron Sirens. She was wearing artsy leggings and a roller derbyin' off-the-shoulder minidress with lacy sleeves and rockin' boots.

She was followed by Anita Coffee in lace-up knee-high boots, funky tights, shorts, and a Morti T-shirt. And after her came Spinning Jenny in a swingy, plaid miniskirt, a Day of the Dead tank top with frilly collar, strappy Mary Janes, and a crocheted beanie.

How did this happen? Why were they here? Was this someone's talent-show entry? Dorothy thought.

Then it dawned on her. These outfits could only have been designed by one person.

Jade tapped Dorothy on the shoulder. "So you like them?" She was wearing a cool T-shirt and a black fedora.

"You designed all this, didn't you?" Dorothy said.

Jade nodded. "Alex's dad, Jerry, helped me sew."

Gigi smiled and put an arm around Jade's shoulder. "So this is what you were doing all that time you were ditching us."

"I had to do something," Jade said. "My mom's had me on lockdown so much lately that about all I could do was hang out in my room and design clothes. I only made it here tonight because Jerry talked some sense into my mom. We worked really hard on this. When she saw how cool the clothes were, she decided to let me come."

"And you got all these models too?"

Jade shrugged. "That was the easy part. They all loved the clothes. Most of them have already placed orders for a bunch of pieces."

Alex and her dads walked up. Jerry and Jade exchanged a high five. "I have even more exciting news for you, Jade. You'll never guess who's in the audience. Louie Veracci, the head acquiring agent at Teen Diva!"

"Teen Diva?" Alex said. "That is the hottest clothing store in the mall!"

"I know!" Jerry said, bouncing on his toes. "There he is!" He pointed to a man in a gray suit with a gray ponytail. He was talking into his cell phone and then held the phone up to show the caller the stage.

When the show was over, Mr. Macarini came back to the stage. "Well, wasn't that exciting?" he asked the audience. "Now if all the contestants can come out from backstage to the auditorium, we'll announce the winners!"

The crowd cheered.

Mr. Macarini disappeared for a few minutes and came back carrying three envelopes. "In third place," he said, opening the envelope, "the Pom-poms!"

The crowd cheered, and a still-soggy Priscilla climbed the stage stairs to claim the third-place ribbon. She feigned a smile, but Dorothy wasn't fooled. Priscilla was not happy.

Dorothy was relieved to hear the Pom-poms were in third. They had a way of winning at any cost. And now that the Pom-poms were out of the way, even if the Slugs didn't place, surely Jade had won.

Mr. Macarini looked at the next envelope. "And in second place, the Slugs 'n' Hisses!"

"Second?" Dorothy said, hopping up and down. "Second! We beat the Pom-poms!" Dorothy sent Alex and Gigi up to the stage together to get the ribbon.

Once onstage, Gigi grabbed Mr. Macarini's microphone. "We may not have taken first, but Pom-poms? This still means you owe us that halftime show!"

Alex leaned in. "On roller skates!"

As Mr. Macarini opened the final envelope, Dorothy squeezed Jade's hand. This was the moment!

"Well, you're not going to believe this," Mr. Macarini said. "In first place by a remarkable landslide, the winner of the fund-raiser money is…"

"Jade!" Dorothy yelled, unable to withhold her enthusiasm any longer.

"Brock Robb and his worm dance!" Mr. Macarini announced.

The boys in the audience went nuts, high-fiving each other, clapping, and whistling.

Dorothy was dumbfounded.

Even Brock Robb looked shocked as he climbed the stage steps and accepted his first-place ribbon from Mr. Macarini.

Dorothy was barely listening as Mr. Macarini asked Brock to tell everyone who he had chosen for his charity.

Brock's voice cracked. "Uh…J. Elway Middle School for, uh, bean burritos. I love bean burritos!"

The audience went wild at that.

Gigi and Alex had returned to the back of the

auditorium now. "So we all lost to the farting worm guy?" she said. "I just don't get it."

Jade shrugged. "Kids love farts more than fashion, I guess."

"Well," said Alex, "on the bright side, the Pom-poms did lose to us. I can't tell you how excited I'll be to see Priscilla and the others trying to dance on roller skates at our big bout."

Everyone laughed. Everyone except Dorothy. Galactic Skate would be torn down now for sure. They hadn't made a single penny in any of their fund-raising efforts. They actually still owed Gigi's mom money. It was all over now.

"Why such a sad face?" Jade asked Dorothy. "You guys beat the Pom-poms. Isn't that great?"

"Sorry, Jade," Dorothy said. "Yeah, that is great. And your show was really amazing. I...I was just thinking about Galactic Skate."

"Oh," Jade said, her face falling too. "The money, right?"

"Sorry to interrupt," said Jerry. "Jade, I want to intro-duce you to someone."

Louie Veracci stepped out from behind Jerry and extended a hand to Jade.

Jade's mouth was open, but she managed to shake hands anyway.

"So you're the young talent that came up with the roller derby collection. Is that correct?"

Jade nodded.

"Well, young lady. You have a very big career ahead of you, and I'd like to have the honor of giving you your first big break. Have you ever heard of Teen Diva?"

Dorothy and Alex squealed, but Jade kept it cool.

"Yes, Mr. Veracci," she said. "Exactly what did you have in mind?"

"Would you girls mind if I had a moment alone with Jade and Jerry?" Mr. Veracci asked.

Still giggling, Dorothy, Alex, and Gigi went out into the hall and waited very impatiently by the door.

A few minutes later, Jade appeared. She had a very serious look on her face.

"What happened?" Dorothy asked, running up to Jade.

Jade cracked a smile. "Let's just say, Galactic Skate is saved!"

Chapter 31

The Undead Redhead, reporting for duty! Dorothy thought, as she opened her sleek, black locker in the brand-new Slugs 'n' Hisses locker room. It was the night of the big state bout against the Steamroller Punks, and Dorothy was actually excited.

Thanks to Jade's generous donation, Galactic Skate's interior had been remodeled with a fresh, modern look. It may have been only a fifteen-thousand-dollar gift, but Jade was in charge, and she used her mad talent for creating designer looks for less to make the skating rink look better than new. Everything was in shades of black, gray, and silver—of course—and Jade scoured discount stores and estate sales for weeks to make the new Galactic Skate hip, retro, and club-like all at the same time. Slugs 'n' Hisses felt new too and ready to kick butt.

They had been training hard for the last month, and their team had grown, as had their skills. Dorothy was sure that they could handle anything the Steamroller Punks threw at them.

But more than anything, she was smiling about the return of Dead Betty. Grandma's hearse had been in the shop for months. It had taken a ridiculous amount of time to order a replacement bumper and exhaust system, and even longer to install them. Grandma wasn't herself without the car. The only upside was that she had gone for three whole months without getting a single traffic ticket. A Grandma record.

Auntie Venom had surprised them earlier that afternoon with a Return of Betty celebration lunch. King crab legs with lots of butter sauce and chocolate cake for dessert. It was the best meal Dorothy had ever had.

But just as Dorothy was pulling her skate laces tight, she noticed something. A rash on her palms.

Not again, she thought, balling her fingers into tight fists. Was this a sign that Eva's curse was back? Everything had gone so smoothly with the restoration that she'd just assumed Eva had been scared away by the sock puppet. Was she back now? Just in time for the bout?

Dorothy tried to push the premonition out of her mind. Maybe this was just another case of nerves. Gigi and Jade were fighting again, after all. In warm-ups, Jade had insisted that this game was too important and too risky to let anyone but her be the jammer. Gigi was furious. She had yelled at Jade, accusing her of being a glory hog, and predicted that Jade would just hurt herself again like she had at the Halloween bout.

"I'm the fastest, aren't I?" Jade had said. "Shouldn't the best jammer be put in? Besides, I saved Galactic Skate. Not any of the rest of you."

"But we're a team, remember?" Gigi said. "And for your information, you aren't the greatest. You're really good, but Alex and Sam are just as good in different ways."

233

That had infuriated Jade, so now she wasn't talking to Gigi. Dorothy would just have to figure out some way to keep Jade in check during the bout. Like Gigi, Dorothy worried that Jade might hurt herself again. And if the Steamrollers were anything like the Peanuts had described, the Slugs already had enough to worry about during the game.

"Five minutes!" Grandma called into the locker room. Max and Angel were cleared to skate into the locker room and wish the team good luck. Dorothy did everything in her power not to look Max in the eye. Gigi was not held back. She stared Angel down and then waved at him wildly, whooping and cheering in his direction as the team skated out.

Dorothy blew her whistle, and fourteen girls in helmets turned to look at her. "Okay, Slugs. You know what we have to do. You know what we're up against. I just want you all to know that no matter what happens tonight, I'm already proud of you." Dorothy paused to look from face to face. "And you all remember what's more important that winning, right?"

"Safety!" they yelled. Everyone except Jade.

"Okay, Slugs! Let's go get those Punks!"

The Quints sped toward the locker-room exit ahead of everyone else, and all five of them wiped out, tumbling through the doorway head over skates.

Just then two girls in short Victorian-style dresses, leather corsets, top hats, and clockwork jewelry peeked in through the doorway, a long shoelace held taut between them.

"Oh dear, Captain Charlotte," said one of the girls with a titter. "It seems we have found ourselves amid falling Slugs 'n' Hisses once more."

"Indeed, Harriet," said Charlotte. "Does it not remind you of something? A talent show, mayhap?"

"Get them!" Dorothy yelled, racing toward the door. It made sense now. The Steamroller Punks, not the Pom-poms, had sabotaged their talent-show performance.

The Steamroller girls skated away, and Dorothy was unable to get past the pile of Quints who were still in a tangle at the doorway.

Jade joined Dorothy in helping the little skaters to

their feet. "Don't worry, Dorothy," she whispered. "I can promise you, there will be revenge on the skate floor tonight."

The poster read: FOR THE LOVE OF DERBY: KISS THIS! SLUGS 'N' HISSES VS. THE STEAMROLLER PUNKS, featuring the new and improved Galactic Skate.

The decimation of the Slugs 'n' Hisses followed...

GIGI GETS A MAJOR BACK BLOCK BY CAPTAIN CHARLOTTE.

JADE IS GETTING PUMMELED ON ALL SIDES AND IS GETTING TIRED.

TALK ABOUT A LOW BLOW! A NASTY BLOCK BY LADY HARRIOT TAKES JADE DOWN.

FINALLY A BREAK. HARRIOT GOES TO THE BOX, BUT IT TAKES JADE AT LEAST FIVE SECONDS TO GET UP.

HOW LOW CAN YOU GO?! A MEAN LOW BLOW TO THE KNEES KNOCKS JADE TO THE GROUND.

And with that, it was halftime.

"This ought to be good!" Alex said, grabbing a front-row seat next to Dorothy.

Jade was on the other side of Dorothy, her skates off, and she was rubbing her hurt ankle. "You really think the Pom-poms are going to go through with this?"

The lights were dimmed, and a single spotlight shone down on the center of the rink. "We're about to find out," Dorothy said, scratching the back of her neck. To her surprise, Ms. Nailer skated into the spotlight, wearing a sparkly unitard. She held a wireless microphone.

"Ladies, gentlemen, Hissing Slugs," she announced. "It is my profound honor to introduce you to the finest roller-skating cheer team in the entire universe."

The audience cheered, and Dorothy looked at Alex and raised an eyebrow.

Alex was so excited that she was bouncing up and down in her seat. "I am so going to enjoy this!"

The spotlight went out, and they heard, "Ready? Okay!"

The lights came back on, and the Pom-poms were in

the center of the rink in a pyramid formation, all wearing outfits that matched Ms. Nailer's.

Priscilla was climbing up the back of the pyramid, and when she reached the top, she stood up.

"What the…?" Dorothy cried.

Alex's mouth was open.

Jade was on the edge of her seat. "She's in skates! How is Priscilla doing that in skates?"

A rap beat blasted through the speakers. "Anything you can do, I can do better," the rapper sang. "I can do anything better than you."

Priscilla leaped into the air as the other Pom-poms rolled out of formation. They came to their feet and caught Priscilla a split second before she would have hit the floor.

"I guess Priscilla is over her fear of skating," Dorothy said.

Circling, they created a spinning flower formation, switched direction, and one by one, did a tight spin and a jump and landed in the splits. From the floor, they smoothly transitioned back to standing and formed a single line, marching in place, fists on their hips.

"Who can do anything the Slugs can do better?" Priscilla called.

"The Pom-poms! The Pom-poms!" they cheered, fists thrust in the air.

"Who can skate better than the Hissing Slugs?"

"We can! We can!" they yelled. "We can can-can!" With that, the Pom-poms wrapped their arms around each other's shoulders and kicked up their skates in a perfectly synchronized chorus-line kick.

The crowd went wild. Dorothy could not believe it. The Pom-poms had not only pulled it off but killed it. The Slugs stared at each other dumbfounded. Dorothy shrugged at the team and began cheering loudly and whistling. The team followed her lead. Every Pom-pom scowled at them and begrudgingly turned to give the team a bow.

Dorothy was stuck behind the blockers now. "Jade!" she called. Pressing forward with a strength she didn't know she had, she pushed between the two big girls. "You have to slow down!" she yelled. Dorothy felt a cold blast of wind whoosh by her.

"What the…?"

Jade looked casually over her shoulder. To Dorothy's horror, Jade's eyes were glazed over like at the séance. "I'm the fastest, the greatest, the best!" Jade called and launched into hyper speed.

"Stop!" Dorothy cried, pushing herself faster than she had ever skated before. "Your wheels!" she shrieked.

"You can't have them!" Jade yelled back.

Dorothy skated even faster.

"You can't take my place, Sally!" Jade called. "Not this time! I'm still the fastest, the greatest, the best!"

Jade was a blur, and Dorothy couldn't keep up. She was out of breath and she was hot. Burning hot. Lava hot. She felt as if strong hands were squeezing her throat. She couldn't get air in.

Then it happened. Jade's wheels flew free, completely disconnected from the skate. Dorothy saw them fly, and Jade was falling. Hard and fast. The arena suddenly became completely silent; the only sound was Jade's head smashing into the track. A sharp, cracking sound.

"Jade!" Dorothy called.

Jade's eyelids fluttered, and she looked at Dorothy with glowing eyes. "You did this," she said, and Jade's body fell limp.

Dorothy's head swam, then everything went black.

Chapter 32

Dorothy's eyes opened a slit. She was staring up at the ceiling in a strange room with pale-green walls. There was a plastic tube across her face blowing cold air into her nose, and a monitor was beeping somewhere behind her head. She looked down at her arms, red and swollen, and noticed a needle taped into her left arm. An IV was dripping clear fluid into her vein.

Grandma's face appeared above Dorothy. "Oh, thank goodness," she said, smoothing back Dorothy's damp hair. "The steroids are finally kicking in."

"Back from the dead," Auntie Venom said, her

face appearing next to Grandma's. "You really are the Undead Redhead, aren't you?"

Dorothy blinked, trying to clear her head. "What happened?" she asked. She tried to sit up, but her body felt like it weighed a thousand pounds.

Auntie Venom looked away and sniffed. "I almost killed you."

"You *what*?" Dorothy said, trying to push herself up again.

"Stay still," Grandma said to Dorothy. "Auntie's exaggerating. It was an accident."

"She could have died!" Auntie said, her voice thin and cracked.

Grandma walked to Auntie and put a hand on her shoulder. "You have to stop beating yourself up, Vanessa. No one knew Dorothy had this. I don't even think she knew."

"Had what?" Dorothy said. Her voice was a raspy croak.

Grandma sighed and took a seat on Dorothy's bed. "You're anaphylactic, hon. Allergic. To crab, we think. The doctor said this reaction was severe though. Usually people don't end up at the hospital without a history of reactions…rashes, that sort of thing."

"Oh," Dorothy said. She had had other rashes. A lot of them, actually. But she'd thought they were stress related, not an allergy.

Auntie had her face in her hands. "I never wanted to hurt you. I never wanted to hurt anyone." Her shoulders were shaking. "I…I…"

"I know that, Auntie," Dorothy said. "It's my fault, really."

Venom turned and looked at her, her eyes wet. "No, it's not. The crab puffs, the jambalaya, the king crab legs…"

"Stop it. Both of you," Grandma said. "If it's anyone's fault, it's mine. Dorothy is my responsibility."

Auntie narrowed her eyes. Her tone was low. "You have to stop doing that, Sally."

"Doing what?" Grandma asked, getting to her feet.

"Taking the blame for me! Protecting me," Auntie said. "It's been eating at me for years. It's time I shouldered the blame."

"But it's not your fault. You were just trying to help her. Save her." Grandma reached her arms out to Auntie, but Venom just turned away.

Dorothy cleared her throat. "Uh, you're not talking about the crab legs anymore, are you?"

Grandma and Auntie both turned to look at Dorothy.

Grandma nodded her head and sat down again on Dorothy's bed. "There's something I need to tell you, Dot."

"Uh, I think I already know," Dorothy began. Grandma didn't need to explain herself. "I know about Eva. And I still love you, but you need to turn yourself in. Or I will."

Grandma's eyebrows scrunched together. "What are you talking about?"

"Oh, uh, I dunno. Usually when someone finds out their grandma is a murderer..."

"Murderer? My heavens!" Grandma said, her hand at her throat. "Where did you get such an idea, Dorothy?"

"The gold wheels. I found them."

Grandma reached for her leopard-print purse. "These, you mean?" She opened the purse and withdrew a silk-wrapped bundle and placed it on Dorothy's chest.

Dorothy pulled back the edges of the fabric to reveal a golden pair of skate wheels.

"How did you—" she started. She thought she had sewn the wheels back in seamlessly.

"I'm more aware than you think," Grandma said with a wink.

The wheels felt heavy on Dorothy's chest. She touched them and felt a wave of sadness and relief pass over her.

"You're doing the right thing, Grandma. If you turn yourself in, maybe the police will go easy on you."

"Dorothy!" Venom said. "Your grandmother is not the murderer."

"But she… These wheels…" Dorothy tried to explain. "Even Eva said Grandma killed her."

Grandma raised an eyebrow. "Eva said what?"

"Eva has it wrong," Venom said firmly, taking a seat on the other side of Dorothy's bed.

None of this made sense. Grandma had the wheels and had hid them. Why would she hide evidence? Dorothy felt like a sandwich with suspicious old ladies for bread.

"You want the truth?" Auntie asked, as if reading Dorothy's mind.

Dorothy nodded.

Auntie leaned in next to her ear. "I did it," she whispered. "I killed Eva."

Dorothy lurched back and the wheels tumbled away. Dorothy's heart monitor was beeping out of control. "You? But that's not possible!"

"Now, Vanessa," Grandma said firmly, returning the wheels to her purse. "Dorothy's been through enough already today. Stop scaring the girl and tell her the whole story."

Auntie sighed. She took a moment to collect her thoughts while Dorothy's heart monitor returned to a normal *beep, beep, beep*.

"Well, Dorothy," she began, "this all started a very long time ago. Back when your mom was a little girl. The geezers—I mean, Galactic Gals—were on this winning streak. Traveling the country...unstoppable. Eva wasn't the captain, you know—your grandma Sally was—but Eva, well, she had star power."

Grandma crossed her arms. "And I didn't?"

"Of course you did, Sally, but Eva, she…"

Grandma sighed, unfolding her arms. "Eva was special."

"So she started to get a following," Auntie continued. "Everybody wanted Eva's autograph. Everybody wanted to interview Eva. And the fame, well, it went right to Eva's head. She was a good skater, of course, but she started to think she was invincible, indestructible. And that is always dangerous."

Grandma shook her head. "The fastest, the greatest, the best."

Dorothy shuddered. She'd heard those words before.

"Well," Auntie continued, "the night Eva died, there was a big exhibition bout at Galactic Skate. What was that, thirty years ago?" Venom asked.

"Halloween night," Grandma confirmed.

"I remember we were playing the Holy Cannoli Rollers," Auntie said, "and there were all these camera crews. Eva was fired up. She'd had her hair and makeup done for the bout, and all these newspapers were taking pictures of her and doing interviews."

251

Grandma nodded. "It was a big deal."

"Anyway, the Cannoli Rollers were one of the best teams in the country, and they had this jammer—gosh, I don't even remember her name now. Goldy somebody."

"Goldy Hahn Solo," Grandma filled in.

"Right," Auntie said. "And Goldy Hahn Solo had done a lot of publicity saying she was going to take Eva out. Bust her chops. Put her in her place. Show her who was really the fastest, the greatest, and the best.

"It was all smack talk, of course. Everybody knew the Galactic Gals were going to win. Not that the Cannoli Rollers wouldn't put up a good fight, but we were ringers. We were going to win.

"Then a couple hours before the game, I saw Moochie and Popcorn follow Sally into our locker room."

"The old locker room isn't there anymore," Grandma explained. "It was torn out sometime after the bout."

"I was worried about your grandma being alone with Popcorn and Moochie in there, so I hid next to the door and listened in.

"Moochie was saying, 'Flip-Flops made some big bets

on the game tonight, see? And the Galactic Gals are going to let the Rollers win. Only problem is, Flip-Flops had this friendly conversation with Eva, and she won't accommodate our modest requests. Now, seeing as Flip-Flops funds your little club here and Popcorn owns this fine establishment, Eva is going to do exactly as we say. And you're gonna make her. You can either take her out of the game or slow her down. Way down. And if she doesn't slow down, we slow her down permanently, capeesh?'"

"You remembered all that? Word for word?" Grandma asked, a shocked look on her face.

Auntie shrugged. "I was paraphrasing a little, but yes, I remember. Anyway, Sally tried to reason with them, but they just stormed out of the bathroom, not even looking back to see me standing next to the door.

"Grandma followed after them, muttering something about Eva not listening to her either, and I knew Sally was right. Eva wasn't going to slow down. Not ever. We had tried to get her to slow down hundreds of times."

"She had a medical problem," Grandma said. "A heart condition."

"I didn't know that," Dorothy said.

Venom sighed. "It wasn't public knowledge. She didn't want to be seen as weak and she didn't want anyone taking her place, so she skated like every game was her last game."

Grandma nodded. "And this game was. Now, Auntie doesn't believe it, but I know it wasn't that crash that killed her. Sure, Eva had a good gash on her scalp and probably a concussion, and there was a whole lot of blood… Oh sorry," Grandma said, noticing that Dorothy was beginning to get woozy.

"What I'm trying to say is that my hand was right over her heart when she died, and that was a heart attack. No doubt about it. Besides I searched out her death certificate after the event, and I was right! But by then everything had simmered down so I let it go. I was so devastated."

"So why did you steal the wheels, Grandma? Didn't the police figure out that it was her heart, not her head?"

Grandma shrugged. "Her gold wheels flew right at me. It was a split-second thing. I grabbed them before anyone saw where they had gone. It's not normal you know, wheels coming off like that. I thought to myself, 'Johnny Flip-Flops did this.' I know Eva blames me for all this, Dorothy. She saw me stuff the wheels in my bra. But I had to hide them before Popcorn or Moochie did. My plan was to approach the police in secret later that night. But I changed my mind after Vanessa told me what she did."

Dorothy looked at Auntie. She looked older somehow. "What did you do?"

Auntie sighed. "I sabotaged Eva's skates. I loosened the action nut on the kingpin. Not all the way. Just enough so Eva would feel her wheels wobbling and slow down. Maybe she'd exit the rink to get her wheels tightened up. Maybe long enough for us to let the Holy Cannoli Rollers win."

"But of course, stupid, ol' me had to go chasing Eva all around the track," Grandma said. "I was yelling, 'Slow down!' But of course, the more I yelled at Eva, the faster she went. Until *whammo!*" Grandma smacked her hands together.

Just like me and Jade tonight, Dorothy thought.

"And so you hid the wheels in my closet?" Dorothy asked.

Grandma nodded. "I actually made that closet to hide them."

"To protect me," Auntie added. "And it's been our dirty little secret ever since."

Suddenly Dorothy knew what had to be done. "I know how to fix this!" she said. "I know how to stop Eva now!" She pushed down the sheets. "Get the nurse. Get Jade! I have to see Jade!" Dorothy stopped cold. "Jade! Grandma, is she…?" Dorothy couldn't say it out loud.

"Oh, honey," Grandma said, taking Dorothy's hand. "I should have told you first thing."

"Told me what?" Dorothy said, her heart-rate monitor racing again.

"She's fine! Jade's just fine."

Chapter 33

A transparent curtain of frost covered the mural on the side of Galactic Skate's wall and sparkled in the cold morning air. *It was the day after the Valentine's Day bout. The perfect day to release Eva's ghost*, Dorothy thought.

The ceremony was all planned out. Dinah and her mom were there. Alex, Jade, and Gigi were in attendance, as well as Sam, Grandma, and Auntie Venom. The mood was serious. Everyone seemed to know that this ceremony had to go just right.

"All ready," Max said, stepping away from the ladder he had just leaned against the mural.

The long crack down the front of the wall had been

filled and patched, but Eva's mouth was still a hole of missing brick. This would complete the Galactic Skate repairs. It would also end Eva Disaster's reign of terror. Hopefully, anyway.

"Here you go, dear," Grandma said, pulling a silk bundle out of her purse and handing it to Dorothy. Dorothy pulled back the edge of the handkerchief. Eva's gold wheels sparkled in the sunlight. They had been cleaned and polished, and Auntie had provided a new kingpin, a replacement for the one she had loosened on that fateful night.

Dorothy wrapped the handkerchief tightly around the wheels and placed the package in Jade's trembling hands. "You okay?" Dorothy said softly.

Jade nodded, turned to the ladder, and began to climb.

Mrs. Gibbs slipped the sock puppet onto her hand and began to chant. "Eva, Eva, hear our plea. Take back your wheels and let us be."

As the chant grew louder, Jade carefully pushed the wheels into Eva's mouth. A perfect fit.

When Jade was back on the ground, Max climbed

up with a putty knife and a small bucket of Spackle. He sealed the wheels inside Eva's mouth as Auntie and Grandma stepped forward, placing a hand on the wall. They talked softly to Eva, explaining in detail everything that had happened that terrible night, how they never ever meant for her to die, how they were forever sorry, and how they loved her and always would.

Once Max had finished the patch, everyone said together, "Eva Dee Setsuko! Forever the fastest, the greatest, the best!"

Dorothy took a step forward, holding her grandmother's hand. "And whenever we play roller derby here," she

259

said, looking up at Eva's face, "we will remember you. We play in your memory and for the sport we all love. You are free now."

"And God bless us all, everyone!" Sam said.

Everyone laughed, and the ceremony was over. Grandma, Auntie, and Mrs. Gibbs said good-bye, and the girls headed inside to grab their gear.

"I'll paint Eva's mouth over the patch when the cement is dry," Jade said once they were inside. "I'll make it perfect."

"Do you think the ceremony worked?" Dorothy asked.

"She said she wanted her wheels back," Gigi said. "That should shut her up."

"But there's only one way to find out for sure," Dinah said. "I'm a roller derby girl. Derby, derby, roller, yeah!"

Everyone joined in. "I'm a roller derby girl. Roller, roller, derby, yeah!"

The lights flickered but didn't go off. Instead, they became brighter. And the newly replaced disco ball started turning as music began playing over the sound system.

Roll on, Sally, roll on along.
I'm glad that you're my mama, so I wrote this song.
No one's gonna get you 'cause you ain't done wrong.
Roll on, Sally, go have some fun.

It was Mom's song! But the words were different.

Just then, Mom appeared at the wall of the rink. She was wearing her cowboy hat. "You like it?" she said.

"Mom!" Sam squealed, skating over to the wall.

"You changed it!" Dorothy said, skating after Sam.

"Well, it's a special version just for your grandma," Mom said. "I realized I've been too hard on her. And I'm sorry. I wanted to make it up to her."

"So that stuff in the song about her stealing the wheels?"

"I know she didn't kill Eva," Mom said. "She's kind of crazy, but she's a good person. And she's a better person now that she's been taking care of you girls. She makes me want to be a better mother too. That's why I've decided to move you and Sam back to Nashville to live with me and Jim."

"Live with you?" Sam said, clapping her hands. "Hooray!"

Dorothy felt like the walls were collapsing in on her.

261

Her wheels slipped and she grabbed the wall to steady herself. "Nashville?" she said.

"And that's not all. I have exciting news. My song? It made it onto the charts! And now that Jim and I are getting serious, I have something real to offer you girls."

"This song?" Gigi said, pointing to the speakers. "Is on the charts?"

"Well, this song, but a different version."

Dorothy folded her arms over her chest. "You mean the one where Grandma is a murderer?"

Mom shrugged. "You gotta understand the country charts, darlin'. Sensation sells. Even Jim thinks I'm destined to be a star."

"Don't stars go on the road and tour and stuff?" Dorothy asked, fishing desperately for an excuse not to go.

"Too early to say," Mom said, "but you could go on the road with me. Be my roadies. Wouldn't you like that?"

Sam was hopping up and down with excitement now.

"But, Mom!" Dorothy complained. "I have a life here now. Friends. I'm captain of a roller derby team!"

"Well, you'll make new friends," Mom said flatly. "In

Nashville. And maybe you can be the captain of some other kind of team. Like the chess team."

Dorothy gritted her teeth. "Chess isn't even a sport."

"So?" Mom said. Her voice was low and annoyed. "The thing is, as nice as Grandma has been about all this," she said, gesturing dismissively around the skate rink, "it was never going to be a permanent situation. You know that. You are my kids, and you belong with me because I love you."

"You have a funny way of showing love," Dorothy spat out.

A flash of anger and then Mom's face fell. "I know this has not been easy on you girls. Probably the opposite, like when I grew up with Grandma. But you are moving to Nashville, Ms. Dorothy Anne Moore, and that is how it's supposed to be." Dorothy didn't have the heart to tell her that living with grandma had turned out to be pretty awesome.

Mom leaned over the wall, kissed Sam on the head, then turned and walked out the front door without saying another word.

Mom's song was winding to an end.

Into the sunset she rides. Bye-bye, Sally. Good-bye.

Chapter 34

Outside, Max was folding up the ladder. Dorothy sat down on the curb and buried her face in her hands. How could she move to Nashville now? Her whole life was here.

Dorothy felt a warm hand on her shoulder.

"Dorth," Max said. He was sitting next to her. "Are you okay?"

Dorothy shook her head. Not okay. Definitely not okay.

"Is this about me?" Max said.

Dorothy shook her head. She knew if she spoke she would cry.

"I'm sorry I've been so distant," Max said. "This Galactic Skate thing has been…a lot."

Dorothy nodded.

"But I have awesome news!" Max said.

Dorothy turned her face to peek up at Max. He was smiling his dimpled-chin smile.

"I got a call a few minutes ago," he said. "One of the Steamroller Punks has come clean about messing with Jade's skates last night during the halftime show." Max sighed and glanced up at the mural. "It's funny. She actually claimed that a ghost woman pinned her down and said she had to tell the truth. Or else. Anyway," he said, looking back at Dorothy, "we've already called the junior roller derby commissioner, and the Steamroller Punks are disqualified. Permanently."

"Really?" Dorothy said. "That is awesome news!"

"And guess what else," Max said, his chocolate-brown eyes twinkling. "The Slugs 'n' Hisses are going to nationals!"

"Nationals? How is that even possible?"

"The Steamrollers are disqualified, so the Slugs are competing in the big bout in Washington, DC, this spring."

"That's great!" Dorothy said. Then her shoulders sagged. "Max?" she said.

"Yeah?"

"I have news too. Bad news," she said. "I'm moving to Nashville."

"Nashville?" Max said. "When? Why?"

Dorothy shrugged. "Soon, I guess. My mom's a big country star now or something."

"But you can't go," Max said, taking Dorothy's hand in his. "You belong here."

Dorothy looked away and willed herself not to cry. "Tell that to my mom."

Max leaned in close. "Dorth?" he whispered.

Dorothy turned her face to his. "Remember what I said about taking it slow and just being friends?"

Dorothy nodded. Of course she remembered.

Max touched Dorothy's cheek

267

gently with the tips of his fingers. "Well, I've just changed my mind."

"You what?" Dorothy said.

"I...I..." Max stuttered. "I...this." He slipped his hands around Dorothy's shoulders and pressed his lips softly against hers.

"Oh," Dorothy said once their lips had parted. "This. This I like."

Acknowledgments

This book series is dedicated to roller derby athletes everywhere—to the geeks, misfits, dorks, brains, class presidents, ex-cheerleaders, prom queens, and class clowns that roller derby loves. Because roller derby embraces diversity, girl empowerment, strength, and individuality, it teaches girls young and old how to love themselves, quirks and all.

Special thanks to everyone who rolled with us and helped us jam through two books in our series. And especially our roller derby community, family, and friends who have supported us on and off the track in our journey, at our events and with our fund-raising.

Love, Meghan and Alece

See where it all began in

Dorothy's Derby Chronicles:

Rise of the Undead Redhead

Chapter 1

Dorothy and Samantha let out terrified shrieks as Grandma Sally gunned the engine, catapulting the hearse over a speed bump and into the school parking lot.

"Are you trying to kill us?" Dorothy squealed.

"Seriously, girls," Grandma said, touching up her orange lipstick in the rearview mirror while steering with one elbow. "You both act like you've never been in a car before."

"Watch out!" Sam screamed, pressing her feet into the back of her older sister's seat. Dorothy looked to the backseat at Sam, who mimed "crazy" by circling her ear with her finger, half smiling.

Grandma swerved just in time to miss a pair of teachers who sprang out of the way, paperwork and books flying.

"Get out of the road, nerds!" Grandma yelled as she tucked the capped tube of lipstick back into her bra.

Grandma's little dog chimed in with a *Yap! Yap! Yap!* through the curtains of the rear window.

"That's right, Morti," Grandma said. "You tell 'em."

"Look, Grandma. There's a spot," Dorothy suggested hopefully. It was a shady space in the back corner of the small parking lot.

"No chance, Dot. Nothing but valet service for Dead Betty," Grandma said, patting the checkered dashboard.

Figures, Dorothy thought. *No one ever listens to me.* She screwed her eyes shut. *Maybe we'll all die before we get to the entrance.* That would teach Mom not to dump them with their nutcase grandma clear across the country.

The car screeched to a whiplash stop right in front of J. Elway Middle School and Grandma pinched Dorothy's arm. "Wake up, chicky. We're here."

Rats. Still alive.

"You can't park here," Sam said, pointing to the large NO PARKING sign looming above the hearse.

Grandma reached into the backseat for her leopard-print purse. "Dorothy and I will only be a minute, hon."

"Um…really, Grandma," Dorothy stammered. "I'm almost twelve years old. I can go by myself."

But it was too late. Grandma was already out of the car, yelling like a peanut vendor at a baseball game, "What you lookin' at?" and, "Take a picture. It lasts longer," to the students filing out of the school bus that had just parked behind them.

Grandma knocked at the window with a ruby-eyed skull ring, her shiny black suit reflecting Dorothy's frizzy red hair through the glass. "Dorothy Moore! Quit fartin' around and come meet your new friends," she ordered, gesturing to the kids she'd just yelled at.

"Please, Grandma." Dorothy's heart was racing. "Let's just go back to the funeral home." She had been living in an old mortuary since Monday, and the last two days hadn't made Grandma's house any less creepy. Still, Dorothy would rather hang out with corpses any day than face the crowd that had formed around the hearse.

Grandma made a disappointed clucking sound with her tongue and swung the car door open. A chilly September breeze swept over Dorothy's bare, freckled legs. She gazed out at the sea of shocked and amused faces and realized she'd made another huge mistake. That morning, Grandma had said it would be "groovy" if Dorothy wore the uniform from her old school, a long-sleeved blouse and plaid skirt—at least until they could buy a new one with the money Mom had promised to send soon.

But these kids weren't wearing uniforms. They were dressed in jeans, classic rock T-shirts with hoodies, cute cardigans with matching boots. Dorothy stared down at her pleated plaid skirt, yellowing button-up blouse, and clunky black shoes.

Grandma tapped her fake nails impatiently on the roof of the car. "Look alive, Dorth."

Okay. I can do this, Dorothy thought. She swung her backpack up onto her shoulder and stepped out of the hearse. But her left foot caught on the car's door frame and she fell forward, both knees scraping painfully on the sidewalk. Cackles and delighted hoots erupted from the crowd. "Frappit!" Dorothy cursed. *So much for first impressions*, she thought, finding her feet and giving the onlookers a little wave and an awkward smile.

"Atta girl!" Grandma said, slapping Dorothy on the rump.

Grandma led the way to the stately front entrance, all the way clickety-clacking on high heels the same hot pink color as her short, spiky hair.

"Why can't I have a normal grandma?" Dorothy grumbled.

Grandma laughed. "Normal is overrated."

Dorothy glanced back at the car. Morti was now in the front passenger seat licking the inside of the window. From the backseat, Sam shook her strawberry-colored pigtails and smirked devilishly at Dorothy through the tinted glass.

"You're next," Dorothy mouthed. McNeil Elementary was only a couple of blocks away. Sam mimed back, open mouthed, "Nooo!" with her hands on her cheeks, shaking her head vigorously.

The gawking mob had grown, and Grandma began waving like she was the float queen in a two-person parade. "Friendly folks," she said, pushing open the heavy front door. "I think you're going to like this school."

Dorothy could already hear the jokes spreading. Kids were whispering things like, "Crazy Granny drives a cursed hearse," and "Watch out for falling redheads!"

As she stepped into J. Elway Middle School, the doors to Dorothy's own living nightmare banged shut behind her.

About the Author

Meghan Dougherty, also known as Undertaker's Daughter with Rocky Mountain Rollergirls, is a roller derby–playing wife and mom and marketing communications professional. Since 2007, Meghan has been entertained and inspired by her roller derby sisters, who are some of the smartest, most independent, and funniest women she knows. Alece Birnbach has been drawing girls her whole life. From her fine art to her commercial illustrations—found on products across the country—Alece has been inspired by the diversity and complexity of the feminine form and spirit. Friends for more than twenty years, Meghan and Alece share a free spirit and entrepreneurial quest for adventure. Together they combined Alece's gift of capturing the essence of sassy girl power with Meghan's roller derby story and adventures, to create a book series for all girls. All to give tween girls a taste of the fun, fierceness, friendship, empowerment, and positive body image that the sport of roller derby brings to women from six to sixty.